Ojai

To Steve

Enjoy!

R.T. Wiley

Printed in the United States of America

Disclaimer
This is a work of fiction, a product of the author's imagination. Any resemblance or similarity to any actual events or persons, living or dead, is purely coincidental. Although the author and publisher have made every effort to ensure there are no errors, inaccuracies, omissions, or inconsistencies herein, any slights to people, places, or organizations are unintentional.

Cover photo courtesy of Shutterstock.com

Cover and formatting: Debora Lewis
deboraklewis@yahoo.com

ISBN: 9781730870286

Ojai

R. T. Wiley

ACKNOWLEDGMENTS

Thank you to my editor Dr. Sally Kennedy.

My wonderful wife Marilyn for her rough draft edits, supports, and love!

To three friends, Larry Tyree, Milt Dodge, and Mike Konyu for their input in the story line.

To Debora Lewis of Arena Publishing for putting it all together

1

It was the year 2000 bringing in the new millennium. It would also be a new start for twenty-nine-year-old Jimmy John Nolan, a Bakersfield California transplant. He moved to Ojai to start his life over after his 1997 divorce from his wife Nancy.

The Nolan family had been long time residents of Bakersfield. Jimmy John graduated from high school and met his soon to be bride at the local malt shop on the main drag through town.

He was happy working in his father's small auto repair garage at the rear of the parent's home. The garage wasn't much to look at but JJ, as his friends called him, was happy eking out a modest living. He would come to work by seven every morning, open up the old wooden garage doors and turn the radio on to KUZZ. He was a Buck Owens fanatic through and through. Blue jeans and cowboy boots and a greasy old Dodgers baseball cap he had owned since high school.

JJ was happy with life but, unfortunately, Nancy was not. Being the wife of a greasy auto mechanic soon wore thin.

"This is not the life I saw us living together JJ." Nancy would tell him. "I want to go out and have fun and go to parties," she would harp.

JJ just took it in stride and tried to pass it off as normal but, after two years of constant complaining he confided in a friend how married life really was, "Not Fun!"

"I can't wait to get to work in the morning and I don't want to come home at night. It's just miserable anymore," he offered. His friend nodded in agreement.

"Look JJ, maybe you need to get away from the garage for a while," the friend said. "I hear Bakersfield Police Department is hiring. Why don't you check it out? It's decent pay and respectable work. You have the temperament and personality for that kind of work. You would be great at it."

"I never thought about becoming a cop. Sounds like it would be interesting work," JJ responded.

Two days later, JJ walked into the Bakersfield Police headquarters and stopped at the front desk area where there was an attractive lady smiling behind a wall of bullet proof glass. JJ bent down and spoke through the pigeon hole and asked about the job. The lady told him to take a seat and the recruiting officer would be with him in a moment.

At 6'2" and two hundred pounds, JJ made an instant impression with the recruiter.

Within days, JJ said goodbye to the auto repair business and hello to the Bakersfield Police academy.

He excelled at the physical part of the rigorous police training program. The classroom portion was more of a struggle. However, twelve weeks later, JJ walked into the unfamiliar squad room where he was told there would be six more weeks of phase training with a field training officer.

After roll call had finished, the duty Sergeant Lance Bentley introduced himself as JJ's FTO and took an instant liking to him. After a short discussion Sergeant Bentley found out they were both Buck Owens fans. He even told JJ he would let him work some of Bucks local events when he finished his field officer training.

JJ was a happy man. He enjoyed his job, and his leader, Sergeant Ed Bentley. Things couldn't be better. Or so he thought.

Mrs. JJ Nolan, or Lady Nancy, as he referred to her, was not so happy. The hours were not only longer, they were weekends and nights. This discontent would fester in Nancy for another year.

One night after working the swing shift, JJ came home to find a note taped to the refrigerator.

"This life may be your dream JJ, but it's not for me by a long shot. I am leaving your sorry ass." Signed Nancy.

JJ struggled along for a while, but he had a heavy heart and needed a change. He loved police work and decided to lateral over to a smaller department in Ojai, California.

~ ~ ~

Officer JJ Nolan was now a proud member of the Ojai California Police Department.

It was much smaller than Bakersfield. The work was pretty much the same but without all the pressures.

The sign on the edge of town stated Ojai Population 9,650 residents. The police department had a Chief and nine officers, one of which was JJ Nolan.

JJ was happy in his new job. He was close to his home in Bakersfield but yet in a more serene environment in the little town of Ojai.

He managed to stay in touch with his former Sergeant, Lance Bentley, in Bakersfield and even went to see Buck Owens on occasions.

Being the new guy on the Ojai team, JJ had the pleasure of working the graveyard shift. Things were starting to look up again. He had worked his late shift only a week when he met a nurse at the local hospital by the name of Turrie Shipley. She worked the graveyard shift as well. Turrie was about the same age as JJ and had never been married. Officer Nolan found himself taking his lunch breaks at the hospital regularly. The two of them became fast friends and started hanging out together. She was an attractive brunette with bright hazel eyes. Her hair dangled playfully about her shoulders. Her strongest feature was her infectious smile.

Ojai was a peaceful town. Usually JJ was the only officer on duty from 11:00 pm until 7:00 am when the day shift came on duty. Most nights, the hardest part of the job was just staying awake. But then, the thought of

Turrie helped. They usually met for breakfast after their shifts.

December 27th, 1999, would become a career changing day in JJ Nolan's life. He had checked on duty at 11:00 pm as usual.

"Ocean 17, I'm 10-8 from the station."

"10-4, Ocean 17, good evening," the dispatcher said.

Another brisk night in the valley, JJ told himself. There were no clouds in the sky and the stars were brighter than normal, or as it seemed.

It appeared to be a quiet night in the little town that JJ had grown to love. He had gone by the hospital, but Turrie was busy so he didn't get a chance to see her. He just left her a note that said, *see you at breakfast.*

Upon leaving the hospital, JJ drove his cruiser down the deserted main street of Ojai. He turned right toward the park. He spotted a black, late model sedan, parked in front of the small playground just off Main Street. The motor was running as indicated by the exhaust pounding the pavement at the rear of the vehicle. The windows were fogged over.

"Ocean 17 traffic," JJ announced into his radio microphone.

"Go ahead Ocean 17," the dispatcher said with her monotone voice.

"I will be out on California 6 David X-ray Bravo 221, black sedan next to the park."

"10-4 Ocean 17, 0:341 hours."

JJ exited his patrol unit and walked up along the driver's side of the sedan. The windows were fogged over making it difficult to see inside. He tapped on the rear passenger side window with his flash light and announced, "Driver, step out of the car."

JJ was a seasoned officer and instinctively put his right hand on his Smith &Wesson 9 mm pistol.

No response.

He repeated his announcement again. "Driver, step out of the car with your hands where I can see them."

Slowly the door opened. The driver gradually raised his hands as he exited the car. He turned and looked JJ directly in the eye. A smile slowly came over his face as a muzzle blast broke through the night's silence. A second person had suddenly appeared from the passenger side of the car and fired two quick shots.

The last thing Jimmy John Nolan remembered was looking up at the sky and seeing three Hispanic males bent over looking down at him as he activated his 'officer down' alarm on his belt. Everything went black.

2

Dispatch immediately called the paramedic team. Her next call was to the Chief and the next in the chain of command, Sergeant Sonny Ulrich. Dispatch gave them the plate and vehicle information. Then continued trying to raise patrol officer Nolan. Chief Phillip Olson sent out an "1133 call" to all agencies that monitored Ojai police band asking for help. CHP and County Sheriff's department each responded.

When the paramedics arrived, JJ's cruiser was the only vehicle on scene. JJ lay twenty feet in front of it on his back with his eyes closed. He had lost a lot of blood. It was determined that one shot hit his vest and the other hit his collarbone and was still lodged somewhere in his body. The Chief and Sergeant Ulrich arrived at the scene at the same time. The medics lifted JJ onto a gurney and placed him aboard their unit. It was code three all the way to the hospital, three miles away. At that time in the morning they didn't encounter any traffic.

Chief Olson radioed dispatch to call out the rest of Ojai police officers and assign them to different locations around town. CHP and the County Sheriff would be looking for the black sedan on the freeways and County roads with the plate number of 6 David X-ray Bravo 221 for the attempted murder of a police officer PC187.

Turrie's shift at the hospital was to the point of being boring. The only thing she had to deal with so far this evening, was a drunk that up-chucked all over her. Later she and another nurse were sipping coffee in the nurse's lounge when the paramedics radioed they were in route with a gunshot victim. They gave his vitals which showed he was in a very serious condition. The medic went on to say their patient was JJ Nolan, an Ojai Police Officer and his dog tags showed his blood type was O positive.

Turrie nearly choked on her coffee and broke into tears. The hospital only had a skeleton crew on during the graveyard shift. Worst of all there wasn't a surgeon on duty, and the nearest one was ten miles away. Turrie pleaded with the head nurse to call him out. The head nurse hesitated, it was 0353 in the morning.

"My God, that's my boyfriend that's coming in! Please don't take a chance with his life! Call the surgeon!" Turrie shouted.

"The only doctor that's on duty tonight is an OB/GYN," the head nurse said in a panic.

They all were running to the emergency entrance.

"Get the O positive blood packets ready in room one, stat!" Turrie ordered.

The OB/GYN got the message about the gunshot victim and was on his way.

"I'm not a surgeon. I won't be of any help," the doc said.

"What if that was your son on his way, would you stand around and ring your hands or would you do your best to save him?" Turrie said with an angry voice.

The paramedic's unit backed into the emergency entrance and quickly unloaded their gurney, calling out the patient's information.

The night air was cold but JJ didn't care.

He was unconscious. They transferred him from the hard board to the bed in room one. Turrie and another nurse quickly undressed him and got an IV inserted into his arm then took him to x-ray. They needed to find where the bullet was in his body. The X-ray showed it was lodged in the tissue just above his heart. As it traveled, it missed his lungs.

He was lucky, the bullet hit the collar bone and broke it, then traveled downward and stopped before entering his heart.

The OB/GYN doctor was preparing to open JJ's chest when the hospital surgeon arrived and took his place at JJ's side.

"Carl, this may be a good time for you to assist me and learn the procedure of removing a bullet," the surgeon told the OB/GYN doctor. "In turn, the next time you are delivering a difficult birth you can give me a lesson."

The operation went smoothly and JJ was out of the woods. Turrie stayed by his side for the next twenty-four hours, continually checking on him.

Other officers had taped off the crime scene and were processing the three pieces of evidence found there, small puddle of urine, two shell casings and a pile of vomit. One officer was taking pictures of JJ's blood that was drying on the pavement.

There hadn't been any response from the CHP or the Sheriff's Department concerning the suspects. By morning, everyone assumed the persons involved were still in the area.

JJ slowly opened his eyes. Everything appeared blurry and it took him awhile to focus. He saw Turrie looking down at him with tears running down her face.

"Honey, you are at the hospital. You were shot, but you're okay now." JJ closed his eyes again and went back to sleep.

There had never been a case in the history of the Ojai Police Department of an officer being shot on duty. It was apparent to Chief Olson how ill prepared they were for such an occasion.

The morning sun was peeking above the mountain top in the distance. The weather forecast was the same as it had been for the last several days, bright dry and hot. The whole nine-man force had been up all night and were struggling with the loss of sleep. A few were able to go home as they were going on swing shift and graveyard later that day.

A couple of two man cruisers were doing a block to block search for the black sedan with the matching plate that was given to dispatch by Officer Nolan.

Ojai was a small city but it had a sizable urban area. Even though the Ojai PD didn't normally patrol outside the city limits it was doing so now. The word spread quickly among the residents what had taken place and who the cops were looking for. Every pair of eyes would be helpful.

The early morning news was carrying the story.

"The police are on the lookout for three Hispanic males driving a late model black sedan with the following license number California 6DX 221. If you spot this car please call 911 and report your information," You could hear the concern in the announcer's voice.

Turrie went home for a couple hours then returned to the hospital to check on JJ. He was awake and eating his breakfast.

"Well, look who's feeling better," Turrie said smiling. She bent down and kissed him on the cheek.

"Is that all I get for nearly getting killed?" He laughed lightly

"Later this evening during my shift when the time is right I'll give you what you want sweetie pie," Turrie said while planting another kiss on his nose.

3

At eight o'clock the next morning, Chief Olson sat at his desk. He knew his small force required help from an agency with seasoned investigators. The Ventura County Sheriff, Milt Ford, left a message with the police department as soon as news of the incident had reached his office. He offered Chief Olson any assistance he and his Deputies could provide. Within minutes, the Chief called the Sheriff's direct phone number. "Milt, this is Phil Olson over at Ojai. I'd welcome your help with this one. We don't have the necessary resources, and with only nine officers and myself we are already stretched pretty thin."

The Sheriff was seated at his desk in his plush office complete with deep-pile carpeting and a large mahogany desk. His wall was filled with certificates from various training courses. He'd been a road deputy for most of his career, and knew what would be required. This was one of those times he and his staff would work together with another agency to find the person or persons that shot officer Nolan. There is nothing like an officer down shooting that will bring various agencies together.

"Phil, you can count on us to put everything we are able to into this investigation. How is your officer?" The Sheriff quietly asked.

"JJ is recovering. His vest stopped one of the rounds, and the other missed vital areas. He is resting, and will make a full recovery. He should be back on the road in minimal time."

Sheriff Ford was relieved. Not only would the officer be fine, but he would also make a good witness. "I will immediately assign my best team to this, and put the rest of our resources on notice. One of our Detectives will contact you within the hour, and start to coordinate with your department."

The Chief appreciated the Sheriff's quick response. He ended the call, and drove to the hospital to see his injured officer.

Detective Captain Zack Vickers, Ventura County Sheriff's Department, received the call directly from the boss. The Sheriff relayed the information Chief Olson had given him. "Ojai PD has requested our help with the shooting incident they had last night. The officer was shot twice, one hit the vest and the other hit a bone but missed any vital spots. He is resting comfortably at the Ojai Hospital, and will return to duty in minimal time. He is awake and responsive, so you talk to him whenever the doctors say it's OK. I want you to head the investigation and use anyone and anything you may need."

Captain Vickers, replied, "Yes sir. Detective Sergeants Ernie Mack and Danny Lenz are my two best investigators. I will get them in here right now." He walked out into the open room and announced, "Listen up everyone. I am certain that by now you have heard about the Ojai officer being shot last night. He will make a full recovery and return to work. Chief Olson of the Ojai PD has requested that we take over the investigation. Sergeants Mack and Lenz will be the lead team. The rest of you will give them whatever help they need when requested. This is now our priority. Any questions? No? Good. Ernie, Danny would you please come into my office?"

The two detectives sat across the desk from their boss. Mack, the senior deputy, looked at Vickers and said, "I guess we need to go over to Ojai PD to check their information and check with our crime scene investigators, talk to the Ojai Dispatcher and meet with Officer Nolan. Anything else for us right now?"

Captain Vickers handed a thin file folder to Mack. "This file contains the sum total of our information. The vehicle information from the license plate on file at DMV. It comes back to a white, 1998 Honda, two-door sedan, registered to Gladys Smith of 625 Oak Knoll Avenue, Pasadena, CA, an eighty-year old, white female. No wants or warrants. Probably not one of our assailants. Our crime scene guys are still working the evidence. They will give me a call when they find something."

Lenz leaned forward in his chair, "Looks like we need to check out Mrs. Gladys Smith and see what her current gang affiliations are. I believe the Latin Lords in

Bakersfield are the most likely bad boys. We've heard they're out and about trying to recruit, but at this point, who knows?"

Captain Vickers eased his six foot five, two hundred-fifty-pound frame out of his chair and walked to the window overlooking the parking lot. "Gentlemen, you know what to do, try to keep me in the loop as much as you can."

The detectives left the office with the thin file in hand and drove to the Ojai police station to make a courtesy call on the Chief, and start their investigation. Lenz drove the plain brown Chevy Impala out of the parking lot and headed for Ojai. The junior member of the team, detective Lenz, glanced at Mack, "You got any thoughts about this yet? Like what is a carload of Mexican gang-bangers doing out in the middle of nowhere at that time of night? Ojai is not an easy place to find. It's miles from a freeway, no restaurants open at that time of night and no Mexican community. They must have had a definite purpose for being there."

Mack was silent for a moment. "Maybe all those points are true, and maybe not. We need to follow the facts."

The next fifteen minutes were filled with silence as each man thought about the case. The drive up California State Road 33 was easy enough at that time of day. The beautiful scenery kept them busy until they made the turn onto State Road 150 at the western edge of Ojai. The grind was about to begin. Within minutes they pulled into the parking lot at the PD, settling for a Visitor parking spot.

No media trucks in sight, Mack thought.

"The officer was alive. No real news here. If he had died, at least he would have made another news cycle. No, nothing to see here." He eased out of the passenger seat and started toward the front door of Ojai Police Department.

The older woman seated behind the extra thick glass barrier looked up and saw the two men wearing sport coats and ties standing at the counter. "May I help you?" she queried in a pleasant voice.

Both detectives thought she was much too pleasant to be working at a police station, but then it was the sleepy town of Ojai.

"Ventura County Deputies Mack and Lenz here to see Chief Olson." Mack announced. He immediately felt a tinge of regret that he had been so formal. They were there to help and she was part of the "family" who had just had one of their own shot and nearly killed.

Before the woman could call anyone, the Chief appeared from a metal door at the side of the waiting room.

"Hello gentlemen. I'm Phil Olson. Thanks for coming." The Chief invited the detectives into the inner sanctum of the Ojai Police Department.

The Chief's office was like any other small town police Chief's. Lenz and Mack could see a large ornate desk with a high-back leather chair that was showing its age. As they looked around they saw high set windows, and walls painted battleship gray. There were several four drawer file cabinets and an over crowded bookshelf. The overhead fan was on full speed and squeaked as it rotated.

"What little information we have doesn't give us much to go on," Chief Olson stated." "JJ Nolan, our officer, is resting comfortably at the hospital. He is still recovering from surgery and no one has gotten much information from him. We have the tapes of his radio transmissions, and some preliminary information from the EMT's, but that is about it. There is a conference room you can use while you are here, and if you need anything just let me know. Now detectives, what can I do for you?"

4

"**S**ince you asked, there are a couple of things you can do for us," Mack said.

"Ask and it's yours," the Chief responded.

"Good. First, we would like the officer's personnel package. We always like to know as much as we can about our victims. You never know when something in a person's past life caused what happened to them later in life." Mack said looking directly at the Chief.

"You think someone may have had it in for Officer Nolan?" The Chief responded with a puzzled look.

"We don't know anything yet," Lenz interjected, "But until we are sure where this investigation is headed, we can't rule anything out."

"Okay, I'll get you the package," the Chief said as he pushed down his intercom and asked his secretary to bring Officer Nolan's personnel file.

"You said there were a couple of things, so what else do you need?"

"Just some background on the mood of the town. Is there anything going on behind the scenes of your sleepy little berg that might have led to the shooting?

Maybe a gang trying to gain a foothold, or a sudden increase in drug trafficking, that kind of thing."

"Nothing I'm aware of, and believe me I would know if we had issues like those. I may be the Chief but we are such a small department I have to pull shifts on a regular basis just to meet our deployment needs, so I am out and about enough to have a feel for the town. I don't know everything but I think I have a handle on the pulse of things."

"I'm sure you do, and I mean no offence when I ask, but we've all been cops long enough to know that there are things that never get kicked up the chain of command for one reason or another." Mack responded.

"You've got me there. I've been guilty of the same thing a time or two during my career. Do you want me to ask around or do you want to talk to my officers individually? I'm good with either. All I want is to catch the bastards that shot my officer, so whatever it takes."

"Figured you'd say that. Why don't you talk to your people and we can follow up if there is anything you think we need to dig into."

The Chief was about to respond when there was a knock on the door and his secretary entered holding a rather thin personnel file. She handed the package to the Chief, then left the room. The Chief checked to make sure he had the right folder then slid it across the desk to the two detectives.

Lenz picked up the file and commented, "Not much here."

"Yeah, Nolan is new. Came over from Bakersfield PD after a divorce from his former wife."

"Any problems in Bakersfield?" Mack asks.

"No or I wouldn't have hired him. We have a unique little community here and the last thing I need is a problem cop. Nolan grew up in Bakersfield and if I remember correctly he married his high school sweetheart. She didn't like him being a cop so they divorced and he moved to Ojai for a change of scenery."

"Is the ex-wife's contact information in the package?"

"Should be, I know she was interviewed as part of our background investigation."

With that, Mack and Lenz stood and Mack said, "If you could show us your conference room and your coffee machine we'd like to review the file before we head over to interview Nolan at the hospital."

The Chief directed the detectives to the coffee room and once they each had a cup of typical cop sludge in their hands they headed down the hall to the conference room and the work began. Lenz reviewed the file while Mack wrote a series of questions on his yellow tablet to ask.

"This coffee sucks, it's no better than what we have at our station. You'd think a yuppie town like Ojai would have Starbucks in their coffee room." Mack commented.

He was about to take another sip of his coffee when Lenz held up his hand.

"You need to look at this partner," Lenz said as he pushed the file to Mack's side of the table.

"Help me out here, what am I looking for?" Mack asked.

"In the background section, Nolan's use of force history while with Bakersfield, PD. He was in a shooting the Chief failed to mention."

"Maybe he didn't think it was important. Was it a bad shooting?"

"On the contrary, it was textbook and Nolan even got a commendation for saving a citizen's life." Lenz replied.

"What are you thinking, revenge maybe?"

"Too early to tell but definitely something we need to ask Nolan about. What say we head to the hospital?"

The two detectives made the short drive to the hospital and found Nolan awake eating lunch. Actually, Nolan was not eating lunch per say he was being fed his food by an attractive young blonde nurse who looked exhausted and worn out. When the detectives entered the room the nurse put down the spoon she had been using and turned to leave. Nolan reached for her hand and gave it a squeeze as she headed for the door.

"I will leave you gentlemen to your cop business," the nurse said as she ducked out the door.

"How did she know we were cops?" Mack asks.

"Maybe it was the cheap suits, or the central casting police mustaches that gave you away," Nolan said with a grin. "I assume you are cops and I'm guessing you are here to see me."

Mack and Lenz stepped up to the bed, introduced themselves and shook hands with JJ.

Mack spoke first, "Pretty nurse, looks like she was giving you the VIP treatment."

"She's a great nurse, she also happens to be my girlfriend, so I hope I'm getting the VIP treatment."

"Girlfriend huh, any reason to suspect a jealous ex out there somewhere?" Mack asked.

"Not that I'm aware of. Wait, you guys aren't thinking I was targeted, are you?

Because my gut tells me it was random. I interrupted something and things escalated."

"It could be that simple," Lenz said, "but until we know more we can't overlook the possibility."

"This is such a sleepy town it would be hard to piss off anyone enough to make them want to kill me."

"What about your previous job in Bakersfield? Did you piss anyone off there?" Mack asked.

"Sure, lots of people, including my ex-wife and my father."

"The ex I get, most of us have one of those, but why your father?"

"Actually, I'm just kidding about my father. He was mad when I quit the family's mechanical business to become a cop, but we are on great terms so no need to go there."

"You know how it is, we still need to talk to him." Lenz said.

"Well if you hang around a while you can. My parents are on the way over from Bakersfield as we speak."

"That's good. It will save us a trip to Bakersfield, that is unless we need to track down your ex. You know what they say about a woman scorned." Lenz replied.

"I'm positive my ex is also a wild goose chase, but I will let you sort that out."

"Okay, we'll let the ex off the hook for now and talk about something else. Why don't you tell us about your shooting in Bakersfield?" Mack asked.

"Not much to tell. Got a radio call about a family dispute and when I got there, this guy was beating the shit out of a young woman. When he saw me, he pulls a knife and puts it to her throat. I draw down on him and start talking as I move closer. I get within a few feet when I see the look in his eyes and I know he's going to cut her. I step to the side a little for a better shot and put one in his forehead. He drops dead and she drops to her knees sobbing."

"Anyone else there witnessing all this?" Mack asked.

"Just my partner initially, but soon the place was crawling with cops and assholes yelling about police brutality. You know the drill."

"Anyone stand out of the crowd?" Lenz asks.

"Well it turned out to be a typical family dispute. As soon as the shooting was over the victim started yelling at me that there was no need to shoot her boyfriend. This despite the fact she had to be treated for a knife wound to the neck. Anyway, she was carrying on and finally some gangster looking guy showed up and the victim was yelling for him to do something. He just looked at me, then walked away. I find out later he was

24

the head of the Latin Lords gang in Bakersfield and it was his younger brother I'd just shot."

"Ever hear from this guy?" Mack asked.

"Not a peep. Then I moved over here to Ojai and never gave it another thought."

"So far, we've got a pissed off ex-wife and a gangster who doesn't like you, anyone else?" Lenz asked.

"Nope, you've got all there is on me in Bakersfield. I got out of there to start over in Ojai."

5

The first Monday morning of the new millennium found Chief Philip Olson in his office at 6:00 am. He was already on his fourth cup of stale coffee. That alone was enough to keep him awake. He found himself staring at the growing stack of papers related to the Nolan shooting when his desk phone rang. He jumped, *I got to get off this nasty coffee*, he told himself.

"Chief Olson," he mumbled into the phone.

"Glad I caught you Chief," the voice on the other end said. "This is Captain Zack Vickers Ventura County Sheriffs Office. My team Lenz and Mack have just been dispatched to the Ojai Meadows Reserve on a report of a dead body behind St. Thomas Aquinas Church. I am on my way now, can you met me there?"

Olson sat up straight in his chair and jotted down the location on his blotter. Minutes later he was out the door and in his unmarked cruiser.

"Ocean 10, in route to Ojai Meadows Preserve behind St. Thomas Aquinas Church. Possible code 8."

"10-4, Ocean 10," came back from the dispatcher.

"I will be switching over to Ventura Chase channel."

"10-4, Ocean 10."

Within minutes, the Chief was turning off of Route 33 and onto a small dirt road that led back in to the reserve, a flourishing wildlife setting popular with hikers, joggers and lovers.

Captain Vickers had pulled up at the crime scene seconds before Olson pulled in behind him. Detectives Danny Lenz and Ernie Mack were already on the scene talking to the witness who had notified the Sheriff's Department.

"I was jogging down the hiking trail with my dog Bingo," Melanie Shuts said, "when Bingo stopped dead in his tracks and wanted to go the other way. He is usually ten feet in front of me and all of a sudden, he heads back the direction we came from. As I stopped to see what was wrong, that's when I saw it."

"It?" Mack questioned.

"The body. It looks like a woman's body, but I didn't go over to it. I just dialed 911 and told the lady what I saw and she asked me to wait for you."

By that time, Vickers and Olson joined the group.

"Before we go any further, I need you to show me where this body is," Mack said.

"I really don't want to go back there!" she said nervously.

"Just take me close enough to point it out, and then the other detective will bring you back here," pointing to Lenz.

Within seconds, Mack radioed back to Vickers that there indeed was a body of a young women and to start setting up crime scene tape.

While Lenz interviewed jogger Melanie Shuts, the Chief and the Captain carefully approached the crime scene for a better look.

"Boss, can you request the forensics team for me?" Mack said.

"Sure Mack. What's your first observation?"

Mack waited a second and then responded. "Hispanic female, sixteen to eighteen years old. A few tattoos, partially clothed. Probably been here several days."

Captain Vickers looked at Chief Olson and before he could utter a word, Olson said, "Maybe it's tied to the Nolan Shooting."

"Can you tell a cause of death or is the body too decomposed?"

"Well, there are three shell casings on the ground about six feet from the body. At first glance without touching them, I would say they are probably 9mm."

"I am not going to touch anything until the forensic team gets here captain," Detective Mack said.

Chief Olson walked over to where Lenz was interviewing their only witness at the moment.

"Do you jog here every day, Miss Shuts?"

"Usually every other day but, since it was a long holiday weekend, I kind of partied down, so this is the first day back."

Chief Olson listened as Lenz continued to interview his witness while they waited for the crime scene unit to arrive. He was joined by Captain Vickers who was busy talking on the radio. When he finished, Olson asked,

"You guys have the shell casings from JJ's shooting, don't you?"

"We do," he responded.

"9mm right?"

"Yup."

"Condition of the body puts it approximately in the same time frame as when JJ was shot, right?"

"To early to tell, but it is very possible. What are you thinking?"

"I'm wondering if the guys who shot my officer had just committed this murder, and was afraid they were going to be caught."

"Definitely a possibility Chief."

Just as Lenz finished interviewing the shaken Miss Shuts, the crime scene investigation team arrived at the scene.

"Good morning," Chief Olson said as Walter Thompson and Sadie Nelson exited their overloaded white Ford van. Whatever was needed, they had it. From ladders to fishing line, they were ready for any occasion.

Walter and Sadie had been a forensics team for little over a year. This was only their second homicide.

"What have we got Captain?" Sadie quizzed.

"Hispanic female, mid-teens, been deceased several days."

"Gee, thanks, you just made my day," Captain, Walter quipped.

"Lenz will take you back to the scene. I would like a preliminary report as soon as you can. I will be here with the Chief Olson"

Lenz led the two crime scene technicians down the hiking path towards the body.

"I guess people will never look at this place the same again. It used to be so peaceful here. Now people will be afraid to come."

"How's your boy Nolan doing today Chief, any update?" Lenz asked.

"Actually, officer Nolan is recovering faster than expected. He wants out of that hospital. He could be back to work in two or three weeks according to him."

As Chief and Lenz continued to chat, Sadie made her way over to the conversation.

"What do we have so far Sadie?"

"Young Hispanic girl, two tattoos. Not necessarily gang tats, but more generic. Typical young Hispanic art. No jewelry, no wallet or purse. Looks like she may have been molested or they attempted and she fought them off. There is residue under her nails and several strands of hair."

"There is one other thing Captain, she had a hand tooled leather belt. We have seen these belts before and they are similar to ones coming out of a little Latino leather shop in Bakersfield. Ernie is going to follow up on that."

She looked at both officers to see if they had any questions. "We will have the body out of here in a couple of hours."

6

Sadie finished photographing the body and the immediate surrounding area. Then she bagged the victim's hands to preserve any evidence. She knelt down next to the victim and attempted to check the girl's pockets. Her jeans were so tight that Sadie had to unbuckle the girl's belt and unbutton the jeans in order to get access to her pockets. Sadie found a folded up one page letter from a Mexican restaurant in Bakersfield in her back pocket. She carefully unfolded it and grabbed the camera to take several shots. The detectives were watching what was going on and came closer to see if they could read the content of the letter.

"What's it say?" Lenz asked.

"It's a letter of termination," Sadie responded.

"Read it to us."

"The letterhead is from Miguel's Mexican Restaurant 1300 S. 43 St. Bakersfield, CA 76802."

Dear Ms. Lisa Delgado,

After a thorough investigation by a private firm, we must inform you that your services are no longer required as of this date. The investigating firm supplied our business with a detailed report along with photographs of your conduct. It showed you stealing cash from the register and food from the kitchen on three different occasions. Signed, Benny Lopez, General Manager.

"There wasn't any sign of an envelope to give us her address," Sadie informed the group.

"I'm sure Mr. Lopez can provide that. We can start from there and work on her background, gang affiliations and family." Detective Mack said.

"Let's have her taken to the Bakersfield morgue, seeing she was a resident there and then have her parents ID her."

"Yeah, sounds good after the forensic team finishes their investigation. Can you call the coroner for transportation of the body to Bakersfield?" Lenz asked Chief Olson

"Sure, not a problem," the Chief replied.

"So, what we have is a belt that we believe was made in Bakersfield, three casings from a 9MM hand gun, an ex-employee of a Bakersfield Mexican restaurant by the name of Lisa Delgado. Did I leave anything out?" Mack asked. Everyone shook their head and didn't speak.

Sadie put the victim in a body bag and asked for help in loading the body on to the stretcher and walking it back to the Coroner's van. The Chief, Captain, Lenz, and Mack each took a corner handle. The terrain was uneven and difficult to walk on until they reached the walking path.

Even encased in a body bag Lisa's corpse was giving off a foul odor that was strongly evident of a decaying human.

"Maybe you should have used a few shots of Febreze," Lenz said holding his fingers to his nose.

Somehow cops can always find humor in a serious situation, and nothing is sacred.

The group each went their separate ways. Mack and Lenz would be heading for Bakersfield. Their first stop would be to notify Ms. Delgado's parents. Mack would call ahead for their address and enter it into the cruiser's GPS.

~ ~ ~

The local news media had a follow up on Officer Nolan. The public now knew he had recovered from his wound and was expected to be back to work soon. That worried Chief Olson. His concern was there may be a second attempt on JJ's life. Especially if it was a revenge hit for the shooting he was involved in while a cop in Bakersfield. Chief Olson confided his concerns with the two detectives before they left.

"It could be we've rubbed up against something that's much bigger, but until we make a run on the brother we are not sure how any of it ties together," Mack answered.

"Until a few days ago our sleepy little town of Ojai was peaceful and serene. Now look at it. We depend on the tourist trade to help keep our economy afloat along with our jobs."

"Yeah, but look at the up-side Chief, if it turns out to be a major drug ring take down or a murder for hire, and we crack the case you can also be a hero."

"I like the way you think, Lenz," the Chief answered.

"Gotta run, Chief."

"Keep me in the loop," the Chief yelled as the detectives sped away.

Chief Olson stopped at the hospital to visit JJ on his way back to the office.

The door was open to JJ's room and he was sitting up playing checkers with the therapist. The Chief stepped in. "How's our patient doing today?" he asked.

"To tell you the truth Chief, he's getting antsy to go home," the therapist answered.

"Only you know if he is ready to go home but I know he's not ready to come back to work yet. The last thing I want him to do is get injured while trying to arrest some drunk and get hurt because he wasn't fully healed."

The therapist agreed by nodding her head.

Turrie entered JJ's room.

"Hi Chief," she said in a cheery voice.

"Hey Turrie, I was just on my way out. See ya later JJ" the Chief said and disappeared down the hallway.

The therapist packed up the checkerboard and pieces.

"I'll see you tomorrow Officer Nolan, we can continue our game then."

Turrie waved goodbye to the therapist and shut the door to JJ's room.

"You're real early for your shift," JJ said.

Turrie looked at him and smiled.

"I just wanted to spend more time with you now that you are fully awake and alert.

Have you talked to your dad lately?"

"He called and told me he and mom would be here later this evening to see me."

"Good, remind me to ask your mom for her blueberry pie recipe. Remember, you said she received a blue ribbon for it at the county fair last year."

There was a knock on JJ's door. He looked up to see his old training officer, Sergeant Lance Bentley.

"Hey Sarge, come on in. I want you to meet my girlfriend, Turrie."

"I had some time on my hands so I thought I'd come by and see what kind of trouble you got yourself into."

"Aw, just a broken collar bone," JJ said smiling.

"Grapevine said you took a couple of rounds," Bentley said looking concerned.

"Just one actually, the vest took the other one in center mass. It caused a little bruising and pain, that's all," JJ quipped.

7

Bakersfield had been an oil and agricultural area for many decades. The city had grown, but it was still a hot, dusty, rough, San Joaquin Valley town. The grit in the air created a brown haze as the detectives came down from the coastal range into the valley. A tough town with many tough citizens, and non-citizens. Mack looked at the GPS and directed Lenz to a shabby section of the city. Broken windows and doors, weeds and bare dirt, trash and abandoned vehicles adorned the neighborhood that had once been the home to Lisa Delgado. They parked in front of the small wooden house that looked like it had been built many decades ago. A screen door provided a barrier, but the front door was open. They heard a Mexican soap opera blaring from a television somewhere inside the house. Lenz rapped on the screen door. He knocked several times before a woman appeared at the door. She could have been thirty or fifty, had dyed blonde hair, too much makeup and tattoos on her arms and neck.

The voice from behind the screen growled in heavily accented Spanish, "What do you want?"

Mack stared directly at the woman, "I am Sergeant Mack and this is Sergeant Lenz from the Ventura County Sheriff's Office. Do you know a Lisa Delgado?"

The woman returned the stare, "I don't know anyone with that name. Now go away."

Mack hesitated for several seconds, "I am going to ask you one more time. Do you know a Lisa Delgado? She's about seventeen years old, and dead." He turned on his heels ready to leave when the woman started screaming and wailing.

"What do you mean she's dead! What are you talking about? You're from Ventura, why are you here?"

Mack turned to face the woman behind the screen door and softly said. "Maybe you could let us in so we can tell you what happened. She is your daughter, isn't she?"

The woman nodded, opened the door and stepped inside. She stood in the center of the room and cried softly. "I knew something was wrong when she didn't come home for the last few nights. She was a good girl. She worked hard. She helped with money." Then a long stream of Spanish that included the words, "Bastard, Asshole, Son-of-a-bitch" and others Mack could not translate due to his limited understanding of Spanish.

When her words finally stopped, Lenz said, "It sounds like you have someone in mind who may be responsible for her situation. If you have any suspicions or ideas we could certainly use the help. Lisa did not deserve what happened to her. She sounds like a good daughter, a hard worker, someone with value."

The woman looked at Lenz with tears streaming down her face. Mack and Lenz noticed the change at almost the same instant. She looked directly at Mack wearing a face of strength and determination. "I don't know any names, but she had been hanging around with some bangers who came around the restaurant where she worked. Maybe somebody at that place knows names. I just know she had started to change after she started working there and met those bangers." She began to cry again. "I need to call my sister and my two brothers. Where is she?"

Mack gave her the name and phone number of the Ventura County Corners Office, and the detectives left the house.

Lenz drove slowly while they discussed the information provided by the grieving mother. "So, we have a good girl gone bad. Maybe we should check in with Bakersfield PD before we stop at the restaurant. Maybe they have a file on the place or its workers. Besides, we should let them know we invaded their turf. We may need their help if things go south. Probably try the Gang Unit to see if the place has any regulars we should consider."

Thirty minutes later they parked at the curb in front of the Bakersfield PD. They put a placard and red light on the dashboard of their unmarked police car. Only a blind man would not recognize the nature of their four-door sedan.

A uniformed Police Officer sat behind a thick glass window reading something. He looked up as the detectives approached the window. "Can I help you gentlemen?"

Mack produced his badge and credentials. "Detectives Mack and Lenz from Ventura County Sheriff. Do you have anyone available in the Gang Unit?"

The officer picked up the phone, "Just a second." He briefly spoke with someone and said, "Sergeant Castillo is on his way."

A door opened to the left of the reception window. A large man filled the doorway and beckoned them in his direction. "Sergeant Ed Castillo, Gang Unit Supervisor," he said. "Come on back with me. You guys are from Ventura County, right? Why in the world would you drive from that vacation spot to this place?"

"Hi Sergeant. I'm Sergeant Ernie Mack and this is Sergeant Danny Lenz. An Ojai PD officer was shot a few days ago, and we caught the case."

"Yeah, we heard about that. The guy used to work here, but went to Ojai for the peace and quiet of a small town, and look what happened. Is he alright?"

"He took one in the vest and another non-fatal to the torso. Got lucky, if you call that luck. He is awake and wanting to go back to work, but I imagine he has a few weeks off."

Castillo opened a door to the gang unit section. The room had about ten desks and no people. The Sergeant waved them into his office. "I imagine you believe the shooter is a gang banger from our little village, or you wouldn't be here. Am I close?"

Mack recounted the details of the attack on the officer, and the discovery of Lisa Delgado. "We stopped at the residence of the late Lisa Delgado and notified her mother. She was not very cooperative until we told her about the death of her daughter. When she heard about Lisa, she immediately started cursing in Spanish, but eventually told us that her daughter had begun to hang with some gang bangers at Miguel's Mexican Restaurant on the South 1300 block of 43rd Street. We stopped by to let you know we are in town and asking questions, and maybe getting some help with the restaurant on any of workers or clientele. We believe it is possible that the guys who shot Officer Nolan are connected to the shooting death of Miss Delgado."

Castillo leaned back in his chair and studied the ceiling for a few seconds. "I know that place. We did some drug buys in their parking lot, but I think we made buys in almost every parking lot in that neighborhood. Let me check our files." He turned to his computer and started searching their database. "Looks like the place is relatively clean, nothing really exciting in our files, but let me check with my guys. They should start showing up in about an hour. Have you guys eaten? I haven't."

Lenz was always hungry, even thirty minutes after he downed a big meal.

"I could eat a horse." he belted out while rubbing his stomach.

Castillo looked at Mack, "Would you guys be OK with Basque food?"

The Ventura detectives had never even heard of Basque food, but they wanted to be polite, and Lenz was hungry. After an interesting meal that satisfied Lenz, they returned to the gang units office. Several officers had already come into work and were sitting at their desks.

8

Castillo introduced the two Ventura deputies and told his crew why they were there. As is usual with cops all over the world, there was some good-natured ribbing about the cushy beach life verses the nature of working in a hard scrapping town like Bakersfield. Soon the banter settled down and the Bakersfield cops gave Mack and Lenz their undivided attention.

"We are looking for some background information on a young woman who was murdered in Ojai. She's Hispanic, from Bakersfield, and she worked at Miguel's restaurant on 43rd street," Mack said.

"Got a name?" one of the Bakersfield officers asked.

"Lisa Delgado," Mack replies.

"Shit," one of the Bakersfield officers blurts out.

All eyes turn to the officer who spoke. Sergeant Castillo said, "I'm guessing there's more to this. So, Abe you want to bring us up to speed on what you know about this individual?"

"I've been chatting up Delgado for the last few months when I stop by Miguel's for lunch. A couple of weeks ago I convinced her to become a snitch. She had good contacts with some of the gangsters in town and I

45

figured she could help us make some cases. I never thought she would end up dead." Abe said.

"I don't remember approving her as an informant." Castillo said, looking at Abe.

Abe slowly opened his desk drawer and pulled out a folder. "I had just finished her background and an informant workup. I was going to give it to you today." Abe said with a sheepish look on his face. "I guess I don't need this any longer." Abe said as he dropped the file in the trash.

"Not so fast. Pull that file out, make a copy for the Ventura guys then give me the original. I'm going to have to bring the Captain up to speed and I'd like to have a little background so I don't look stupid. I just hope you haven't been sitting on this, and I really hope that your relationship with Miss Delgado was strictly professional, and by professional I don't mean you were paying her for anything but meals." Castillo said.

The men snickered and said, "Yeah buddy"

"No.., honest boss, I never talked to her without my partner Ricky being present. It was all legit."

There was more snickering and hoots from the rest of the crew, but Castillo quickly brought a halt to the banter. "Just make a copy of that file so the detectives can be on their way. I'm sure they didn't drive all the way to Bakersfield to listen to our internal issues." Castillo said as he looked at Mack and Lenz.

By now the room was silent and Mack was the first to speak. "Any chance we can speak to your guys about their meetings with Delgado?"

"Not only is there a chance, I'm going to insist on it, but only if I can sit in on your meeting." Castillo said.

"Not a problem," Mack answered.

Castillo stood up from his desk and told the rest of the crew to hit the streets. Within minutes the squad room was cleared, except for Lenz, Mack, Castillo, Abe and Ricky.

Castillo sat at his desk and the other four pulled their chairs over close to his desk.

"Before we go any further I want my guys to know that I am assuming that they did everything by the book. This is not an investigation into their activities but rather they are assisting another jurisdiction with a murder investigation. If we cannot agree to those terms we don't talk. I don't want the Captain or their union saying we conducted some sort of witch hunt here."

"Mack and I are good with that," Lenz said as he looked at Mack and they both nodded.

"Okay then. Why don't you tell us about Miss Delgado and how she came to be an informant?" Castillo said.

Abe starts out, "Lisa was a good kid who was starting to slide down the slippery slope into a life of drugs and gang banging. When we first met her, she was pretty innocent. She'd been around gangsters growing up but had managed to avoid becoming too involved in the lifestyle."

"What about recently?" Mack asked.

"Things started to change a few months ago and she showed up with some gang tattoos and started talking all tough and shit, like she was into the lifestyle, you know." Abe said.

"It got to the point where we didn't feel comfortable eating in her section anymore." Ricky chimed in.

"Then a couple of weeks ago we ended up seated in her area and she asked us what we could do to protect her if she gave us information on some bad dudes. I told her this was not like some TV show where the Feds swoop in and whisk her off to a witness protection program but if she worked with us we would do what we could to keep her safe."

"Did she ever give you anything good?" Lenz asked.

"No, we met her one night away from the restaurant so we could get the information we needed for our informant package and she told us rumors were floating around that something big was going down soon, but she had no idea who was involved or what it was." Abe said.

"Did you see her again after that?" Mack asked.

"Only once and she seemed scared." Abe answered.

"Scared, in what way?" Lenz asked.

"She kept looking around like she thought someone was watching her, and she barely talked to us. If you ask me something had her spooked." Abe said.

"Sounds like maybe she got in the middle of something and it ended up getting her killed. I'll have my guys start beating the bushes to see if we can find out what's going on." Castillo said.

"Does that include rounding up the usual suspects?" Mack asked with a smile.

"It does," Castillo replies. "We always start out by rounding up the usual suspects."

All five men laugh at the movie reference.

"Well, we should head back over the hill and leave you to your job. Keep us posted." Mack said, as he and Lenz stood, and did the hand shakes all around, then they headed out the door.

Once in the car Lenz turned to Mack and said, "Think Castillo and his people can turn up anything that will help us solve this one?"

"My gut tells me that it started in Bakersfield and progressed into Ojai, where it just happened to be a safe dumping ground for the unfortunate Miss Delgado. I'm also guessing that her murder and the shooting of officer Nolan are related, and if we solve one we solve the other."

"I think you're probably right on that partner. Now let's get the hell out of this dry, dusty town and head back over the hill to God's country."

9

Turrie and an orderly entered the hospital room with a wheel chair.

"Well, it looks like you made bail." Doctor Singh said. "You can go home now, but no work for at least thirty days."

"Fat chance," JJ blurted out.

"No, I'm serious. You are going to obey doctor's orders or I will have Chief Olson drag you right back here to the hospital where I can keep an eye on you. You stubborn jerk." Turrie responded.

"Now, now, my mother would not like that kind of talk," he said with a chuckle.

"Speaking of mother, my parents want me to come back to Bakersfield with them for a week or two while I am recouping. If I do, why don't you come up on your days off?"

"I'll have to think about that," she grinned. "Now, get your fanny in this wheel chair and I will take you down to discharge so you can sign your release papers."

After bidding the staff farewell and thanking them for their care, Turrie and the orderly wheeled JJ out of the sliding glass doors to his parent's waiting SUV.

"Here he is Mrs. Nolan, signed sealed and delivered."

"Thank you my dear. I am so grateful for all you have done for my boy."

"Not a problem. I had a special interest in this patient you know," she giggled.

JJ stood and eased himself into the backseat of his parent's vehicle.

"Turrie, please come over and spend some time with us. We have plenty of room and I am sure this rascal will be like a caged lion in two days," Mrs. Nolan said.

"I would love to." Turrie responded as she returned to her other duties.

"What a beautiful day," Mrs. Nolan said as they pulled away from the hospital. I am so thankful to be taking you home for a few days. It will be just like old times."

JJ rolled his eyes and smiled at his mother.

"By the way, Sergeant Bentley has called several times to get a progress report. He wants to come by the house and see you when we get back. Are you up to that?" JJ's father said.

"Absolutely. I feel great. Besides, I want to talk to him about the Delgado case. I remember that little girl from the projects when I was in Bakersfield. I used to know her big brother, Tommy. He was one of the few who grew up and got out of the projects and away from the gang bangers."

They pulled up in front of their aging family home on Fry street. JJ looked around at the old neighborhood.

Things had deteriorated a lot since he left the family business. His parents were now in their late sixties and had no intention of leaving the family home of thirty years. JJ's dad still dabbled in his garage at the rear of the property, but working on cars in this day and age was not something he could readily do. Now bring him a 57 Chevy and he could take it apart and put it back together blindfolded.

The garage was now leaning distinctly to one side and to JJ's dismay, graffiti had been sprayed on the sagging front doors.

"Dad, there is gang graffiti on the garage! When did that happen?"

"Oh, a few weeks ago. It's happened a couple of times, so I just paint over it. It's getting to be too much work."

When they exited the car, JJ knew immediately what the graffiti said and where it came from. It was the Latin Lords and it specifically said in Spanish "Salir de nuestra calle." Leave our street.

JJ didn't say anything in front of his mother but quickly cornered his dad when they got into the house.

"Dad, I know you very well, you speak enough Spanish to know what that means. It's time for you and mom to put this house up for sale and leave this neighborhood. You both deserve to live in peace and enjoy life. You shouldn't have to be looking over your shoulder all the time or sleeping with one eye open at night."

"Son, we are old. We raised our family in this house. We have seen all the ups and downs of our life here. No one is going to run us off now."

JJ just shook his head. He knew his pleas were futile.

"Now, not a word in front of your mother. She is just happy you are here and safe."

JJ grabbed a Coke out of the refrigerator and walked out the back door to take a closer look at the garage. For the first time, he felt bad about leaving Bakersfield and not being here to keep any eye on things. He was worried about his parent's safety, but he also knew he would never convince them to move.

Sipping the cold bottle of Coke, he decided to go into the old shop he had grown up with and look around for old time sake. It was just like old times, drinking Coke from a bottle. His Dad would never have Coke in a can and insisted that his mom always buy bottles. That probably goes back to the old days when there was a beat-up old red Coke machine in the shop. Twenty-five cents a bottle for all of the Nolan Garage customers.

As JJ approached the side entry door of the old structure he noticed that the hasp and lock had been ripped off. When he got inside, he was heartbroken. All of his dad's tools were either missing or destroyed.

The Latin Lords weren't playing around. They were serious about getting his parents out of the neighborhood one way or another.

Just as JJ left the garage, a black and white unit pulled in the driveway.

"Hey Sarge, how you doing?"

"I'm fine JJ, the question is, how are you doing?" Sergeant Bentley shot back.

"I think I could run a mile and clear a six-foot fence, but my doctor won't give me a release for thirty days. Make that twenty-nine."

They both laughed and sat down on the front porch to catch up. Mrs. Nolan poked her head out the front door and said she would bring them some ice tea.

"I wanted to ask you about the Delgado case, but when I got home, I was more concerned to see the graffiti on the garage. When I went inside, it looked like a bomb had gone off in there. I tried to talk to my dad about getting out of here, but he won't budge," JJ said.

"Gang activity has grown two-fold since you left here."

"Who is president of the Latin Lords now?"

"Eddy Gallegos. He's the older brother of the banger you shot when you were with Bakersfield P.D. Eddy took over and has been seeking revenge ever since. I would expect his name will come up as a suspect in your shooting as well."

"Any ties to the Delgado girl?"

"Grapevine said he was trying to use her to transport drugs up from L.A. and she didn't want any part of it. That was a week or so before her body was found."

"Eddy is a sharp guy. I doubt that he would have killed the girl himself, but he has the power in the gang to have someone else do it as part of an initiation or something."

"She was a nice kid as I recall, sorry to hear all this."

"Guess it won't hurt for me to be around here for a few days to get the lay of the land again." JJ. said.

10

"**D**ad, when was the last time you were in the shop?" JJ asked.

"Day before yesterday when Walt Newman brought his old 40 Ford classic in to have me replace his old transmission with a new TH700 automatic. I'll have to pull the engine tomorrow and order a new one today. It will be here tomorrow from Los Angeles. Why do you ask?"

"Dad, come with me."

They walked out to the garage together and JJ opened the door. The old man noticed the lock and hasp was missing. They stepped inside and Mr. Nolan stared at what had happened to his shop. All his major tools were gone but most of all so was Walt Newman's old classic Ford.

"Oh my God!" What have they done?" Mr. Nolan spoke in a whisper. Tears ran down his cheeks and he began to shake. JJ held his dad by the shoulders to steady him. The older man turned to face his son and hugged him.

"JJ, I'm afraid for your mother. I don't think I would be able to protect her if those people came back."

"Don't worry Pop, I'll make sure Sergeant Bentley assigns extra surveillance to the neighborhood. At least as long as it takes you and mom to move. Maybe you could move to Ojai, it's a great place to live," JJ said as he winced from pain around his mending collarbone.

"What will I do about Walt's 40 Ford?" Mr. Nolan asked as tears welded up again.

"Do you have any insurance Dad?"

"I think it lapsed a couple years back, Son."

"Call Walt and tell him what happened. You guys have always been good friends. Maybe he has insurance coverage on the car," JJ responded.

"I left the keys in the ignition like always," Mr. Nolan said.

Mr. Nolan told his wife what had taken place in the shop. She held her hand over her mouth and starred back at him.

"They want us out so badly. I'm afraid they may set fire to our place next time," Mr. Nolan said.

"That was exactly what I was thinking too," JJ said with a concerned look.

JJ's father picked up the phone and dialed Walt Newman's number.

"Walt here," a voice said loudly.

"Glad I caught you home," Mr. Nolan said.

"Did you get the car finished already?"

"No Walt. I got some bad news. Someone broke into my shop and stole your car and all my tools last night."

"Oh...my God! that's awful news. When did you find out about it?"

"Just a few minutes ago when JJ and I went to the shop."

"You call the cops yet?"

"Well there's one at the house right now."

"Do you have insurance on your shop?" Walt asked.

"No, sorry to say I don't."

"Do you have coverage on your car?"

"Yup, sure do, don't worry about my car. Maybe I'll get more back than I have into it," Walt said laughing. His good nature made Mr. Nolan feel a little better.

Walt Newman had lived his whole life in Bakersfield and had always been involved with cars. Sometimes he would race them and other times he built them. Walt was president of the local classic car club. He put out the word about what happened to his 40 Ford and Mr. Nolan's shop. Most of the club members had Mr. Nolan work on their vehicles at one time or another.

"Dad, Sergeant Bentley has called a unit to take a report from you and Mr. Newman about what was taken, they should be here in a few minutes."

"Okay son, I have to call and cancel the transmission order."

JJ.'s parents walked out to the front porch and sat on the swing and waited for the Bakersfield PD to arrive. The thought of leaving their old neighborhood was saddening for them as they looked around.

"Lots of good memories," they said together.

A caravan of three low rider cars drove by with several angry Mexicans in each car shouting obscenities and showing gang signs. It didn't bother them that

Sergeant Bentley's cruiser was sitting in the driveway. JJ heard his dad shouting at someone. He and Sergeant Bentley ran to the front porch as the cars sped away.

JJ decided he was appointing himself as sentry for his parent's home. He planned on going to bed early and staying awake from eleven to seven in the morning. His tools for combat were his flashlight, a baton, his service weapon and a stun gun.

His parent's phone would ring early in the morning. When they answered, a Mexican voice would say in Spanish, "You will die." The caller made it a point to call at different times, but always the same voice.

Eddy Gallegos called a meeting of the Latin Lords at their clubhouse. Ten of his top soldiers attended.

The gavel hit hard on the tabletop. "Meeting come to order!" he shouted.

"How many of you were in our caravan yesterday when we did a drive by the Nolan's house?" Six members raised their hands.

"Did you see who was on the porch? It was that asshole JJ. The one who killed my brother. We don't have to go to Ojai anymore, he's been delivered to us right here in Bakersfield." The members raised their hands with gang signs and shouted "Death to JJ," in Spanish.

"I'm putting a $1,000.00 bounty on his head, to whoever kills him. Pass this on to the rest on our members" Eddy said proudly. The meeting was over. It was time for drinking and planning on how and when to kill Officer JJ Nolan. Several gang members offered their suggestions, but Eddy wanted that pleasure for himself.

11

Sergeant Bentley and the responding officers had driven away from the residence. JJ felt very alone, more so than ever before in his life. The police would increase their patrols, but he knew that was really no deterrent. The smart thing to do was to get his family out of there, and quickly. He thought about installing surveillance cameras around the property, but that would not stop a drive by shooter.

The Bakersfield PD Gang Unit had reported to work. Several hours into the shift, Sergeant Castillo was reviewing Patrol Division incident reports from the day shift. He went through this ritual every day. On more than one occasion he identified an incident that would signal some later gang action. Nearing the bottom of the stack of reports, he noticed a theft report from the Latin Lords home turf. At first, he did not recognize the Anglo victim, but he knew it must be one of the old white holdouts from the past. Several of them had not moved during the change from White to Hispanic. Then it hit him. The name was Officer JJ Nolan, formerly of BPD. The report referenced Sergeant Bentley. He picked up the phone and called Bentley at his home since he had completed his shift. Bentley answered and gave Castillo all the details of the situation. After the call had concluded, Castillo began to think about several possible scenarios. All of them ended very badly for the Nolan family. He called the members of his unit and directed their return to the office.

An hour later, the entire Gang Unit had assembled in their office. The Boss had not given them any information or instructions. He did not want this to leak out to anyone.

"OK guys, this is what we have." He recounted the auto theft and stolen tools from Mr. Nolan's garage, the drive-by and the history of Officer Nolan with the death of the former President of the Latin Lords. "We all know what these little assholes are like, and what they can do. We need to find out what these cockroaches are up to. Maybe it is just typical words and tagging, but it might escalate. This is our gang against theirs."

Some of the officers started making phone calls, and some went out on the street to make personal contact with their sources.

~ ~ ~

Eddy Gallegos was sitting at his desk in the Latin Lords clubhouse when one of his gang members came into the room. The banger was a skinny kid, not much over five feet tall, with soft eyes and a quiet voice. He looked like he should be serving as an altar boy at St. Thomas Catholic Church, but his mind was more into the world of Lucifer. He was totally immoral and had no compunctions about either quick death or torture resulting in death. He enjoyed either option. "Jefe, I know how much you loved your brother. May I have the honor of killing this Gringo Pig as a gift?"

Eddy eyed the kid as he stood in front of the desk. "You may do whatever you wish. You have served your brothers and me well in the past. But I will not stop the others from trying. Do you understand?"

The Kid did not understand, but he nodded in agreement, and walked out of the house to his bicycle and rode away..

The Gang Unit had been working their snitches for several hours, but, so far, they hadn't discovered anything. Castillo had remained in his office. He knew his officers would give him a heads up as soon as they knew anything. His private cell phone started buzzing. Only a few people had this number. When someone called, it was either family, or a very small group of trusted friends. "This is Castillo."

He immediately recognized the voice on the other end.

"Ed, we are not having this conversation. We have been running a wire on the Pasadena Latin Kings in our jurisdiction, without any results. That was until some banger from the Latin Lords in your town called his cousin down here, telling him he has a chance to make an easy thousand dollars. Our guy asked, "Where you gonna get a grand?" Your guy said he is going to kill some cop the Lords wanted dead, as a payback for offing the Jefe brother awhile back. That's all I have on this, and can't give you any more right now."

The call had ended before Castillo could say a word. He put the phone down, and called his unit back to the office.

His team was back at their desks. Castillo came out of his office, stood in front of his officers and said, "I just got a call from a reliable source that the Latin Lords are going to kill a police officer as a payback for that officer killing the brother of Eddy Gallegos awhile ago. Whoever gets the job done first would earn a thousand dollars. Have any of you heard anything about that from the street?"

The officers looked around the room. No one had anything to report. Castillo recounted his review of the reports, the phone conversation with Sergeant Bentley describing the details of the threats and the dead girl found at Ojai. The unit listened with growing concern. One of the officers asked if JJ was aware of the threat.

"Not yet. We have two cars on patrol in the area, and JJ is armed. That's it for now. Get to work." The Gang Unit officers made more phone calls and went out to make more informant contacts. Castillo drove out to visit JJ.

The skinny gang banger got on his bicycle and rode to the Nolan's house. The kid melted into the scenery. His baggy shirt concealed his Glock pistol. His "baby-face" concealed his true unbalanced psychological illness. He loved to kill with no remorse. He had done it before. Even after his first kill, a ten-year old member of another gang, he felt nothing. He had never really been a highly visible member of the gang. Even the Bakersfield cops didn't consider him much of a threat. He kept riding his bicycle.

Castillo was in his worn old pick-up truck driving to see JJ. He was lost in his thoughts as he drove to within two blocks of the Nolan residence. Without any warning, a skinny Mexican kid rode his bicycle in front of his truck. Castillo slammed on the brakes. The truck slid to a stop only a foot from the bicycle. The kid looked up, his eyes wide and full of panic. Castillo looked directly at the kid. They stared at each other for an instant, then the kid sped off in the opposite direction and disappeared.

The kid stopped in an alley behind a garage and took a deep breath. He had just cheated death, but in a most pitiful way. How would it look for someone like him to be killed by an old pick-up truck while riding a bicycle? Not a very glorious end for a banger, plus he could use the money he would earn for killing the cop.

Castillo was returning to normal. His breathing and heart rate had slowed. He never saw the kid before he nearly became a hood ornament, but his face had been burned into his memory. Castillo drove slowly to the Nolan residence. He parked a few houses down the block, and walked back to the Nolan's house while keeping an eye out for any suspicious activity. He was aware that he could be a target himself as he continued his walk.

12

JJ was on the alert and noticed Castillo heading up the sidewalk. He met him at the door. The two knew each other from JJ's tenure on the Bakersfield PD so their meeting under the current circumstances was bittersweet. It was great to see each other again and maybe have a chance to catch up, but clouded by the fact that this was not a happy time for the Nolan family. After a quick handshake JJ and Castillo headed to the kitchen to talk in private.

Castillo spoke first, "Now that you've seen what's going on around here, what are your plans?"

"If this was just about me, I'd stay and dare those assholes to try and drive me out of this house. But I have my Mom and Dad to think about so I want to get them out as soon as possible."

"Good idea. I hate to see anyone cave in to these punks but I think you are doing the right thing."

"It may be the right thing but it still sucks and it sure doesn't make the problems any easier for you guys. We both know any victory for the gang only emboldens them and allows them to attract more young kids into the lifestyle. They need to be hurt big time so the reality of life in a gang hits home with some of the want-to-be bangers. Instead I feel like we are handing them a victory they can hold aloft like some kind of fucking trophy."

"I hear you brother, but your parent's safety has to come first, so you're going to have to let them win this round. Our time will come and when it does I promise you we will bring the full weight of my unit down on their little pointy shaved heads. So, what are your plans?" Castillo asked.

"I've got movers coming tomorrow to clean out the house and put everything in storage until we figure something out long term. That will get my parents out of the neighborhood and hopefully out of danger."

"That's a good start but what about the house. You know the gang will move in as soon as you're gone and use it as a base to expand their hold on the street. You will never be able to sell it."

"Yeah, I thought of that. If it were up to me I'd booby trap the place then let the dumb fuckers have it."

"I don't want to be hearing that, although I like your style."

"Don't worry Sarge, I wouldn't really take things that far. I've thought about it but couldn't figure out a way to only kill the bastards I wanted dead. My luck a couple of innocent kids would wander in and set things off. No, I have another plan."

"Legal I hope."

"Mostly."

"Do I want to know?"

"Actually, I am going to make your job a little easier. After we say our goodbye's I was going to have the place bulldozed and just leave the pile of rubble behind. But that seemed like a waste so I decided to donate the house and land to the Catholic Church with the stipulation they use it to house the nuns from St. Elizabeth's Parish. One of the reasons my parents stayed in the house was because the church was just around the corner. I figure even hardened gangsters will draw the line at harming a nun so their presence may make the neighborhood a little safer."

Castillo laughs, "I'm sure the hard-core bangers are beyond saving but it just may keep some of the want-to-bes away. Can't wait to see what happens. Until you move out, anything you need from us?"

"The beat cops will have extra patrol units in the area, and I will remain here until we leave, so I think we're good." JJ said.

"Oh, by the way the reason I came to see you is, we've learned there is a thousand dollar hit posted on you by the Latin Lords. Keep your head down and be safe."

"That's all I'm worth, a measly one grand?" JJ laughed.

"You know if you need anything me and my boys are only a phone call away."

"I appreciate it Sarge but I think we will be fine for one more night. My big problem is getting my parents to adjust to the move. They are leaving behind the home they have shared most of their married life. I was raised

71

here and my Dad ran his business out of here so it will
be tough."

"Sorry I can't help you there. It sucks the way things
turned out but you are doing the right thing. Safety first,
that's my motto."

With that Castillo stood to leave. He and JJ walked
back into the living room. Castillo said good bye to Mr.
and Mrs. Nolan then turned to leave.

"Nice meeting you Sergeant," Mr. Nolan said, "Sorry
we had to meet this way."

Castillo turned to face Mr. Nolan, "It's a shame
things turned out like they have. I wish there were more
we could do but the law frowns on my just taking the
punks out and shooting them."

"Look, I know it's not your fault, but it is too bad
that people like us have to give in and leave our homes
while the hoodlums stay. It's just not right," the old man
said.

"You're preaching to the choir. The system is broken
when the criminals have all the rights and the good
people have to live in fear. We fight an uphill battle to
keep the streets safe and all I can tell you is we will do
our best to see that these gangsters get what is coming
to them someday." Castillo replied.

Castillo walked out to the porch and JJ joined him.

"As you can see my parents are a little frustrated
right now. They will move on with their lives but now
they simply want some justice." JJ said.

"Don't we all," Castillo replies. *It always seems like the bad guys get the breaks and the law biding citizens get the shaft.*

As Castillo started down the steps the same kid rode by the front of the house on a bicycle. He appeared young and innocent like he didn't have a care in the world. Castillo noticed him and waved.

"Know him?" JJ asked.

"Never saw him before today. I almost hit him on my way here. He rode his bike out into traffic and it was close. I remember him because he didn't make a big deal out of it like some of these kids think they have to do to prove their machismo. He just smiled and rode away. Maybe there is some hope for people after all."

"Who knows," JJ said as he turned and headed into the house.

Castillo walked to his truck and was about to get in when the kid on the bike rode up.

"What's up youngster?" Castillo said in a friendly voice.

"Fuck you, you lousy pig," the kid said as he pulled out his pistol and fired two rounds into Castillo chest.

The kid stuck the pistol back into his waistband, looked down at Castillo gave him the bird, and rode off.

13

JJ had just walked back in the front door of his parent's house when he heard the two very unmistakable gun shots fired in rapid succession. He froze for a second into a half crouched position and then turned and hustled back out the front door and looked both ways up and down the street. About twenty yards away, he saw the limp body of Sergeant Castillo laying on the ground next to his undercover pickup.

JJ ran to Castillo's assistance. He noticed right away that Castillo wasn't wearing a vest and was losing blood rapidly. JJ looked up and saw the little asshole on the bike speeding away around the corner.

He grabbed Castillo's radio from his back pocket and keyed the mic. "Triple nine, triple nine, officer down!"

In less than ninety seconds, the neighborhood was swarming with Bakersfield officers rushing to Castillo's aide.

JJ worked frantically trying to get a pulse on the, now still body, of the man he had just had a conversation with some five minutes earlier.

Another two minutes and paramedics arrived and took over the attempt to bring the poor sergeant back to life.

"Who did this JJ? Who shot Castillo? Did you see who it was?" The first cop on the scene asked.

"Na, some little fucking gang banger." JJ answered.

There was chaos up and down the formerly quiet street. People had come out of their houses as cops arrived on the scene. Everyone wanted to know what happened.

It wasn't long until the news media showed up as well, trying to intrude on the murder scene as only they can do. Dumb jerks.

"This is a crime scene, leave now," one of the officers told the pushy reporter. "Now!"

Sergeant Bentley hurried to where JJ was still kneeling on the ground next to Castillo's body.

"What happened JJ?" he said with mounting anxiety in his voice. "Castillo was a good friend of mine." Sergeant Bentley said.

"I think those bullets were meant for me Sarge," JJ said shaking his head. "Castillo came by to give me a heads up that the word on the street was there's a price on my head. Whoever shot Sergeant Castillo, must have thought he was me," he said in a very distressed voice.

By then, the Chief of Police and all of Castillo's gang unit officers were on the scene. It was all the Chief could do to keep the loyal Castillo team from declaring open season on the Latin Lords.

"After I heard the two shots, I saw this skinny little Hispanic kid riding away as fast as he could pedal. He turned left at the corner and then I lost sight of him," JJ said.

"Description?" the sergeant asked. We need to get an APB out as quick as we can."

"He was a skinny little bastard," JJ. responded. Looked really young, maybe fifteen to sixteen years old. Hispanic, light complexion with really short hair. He was wearing a white t-shirt with sleeves cut off and blue jeans. I could see the gun tucked in the back of his pants as he turned the corner." JJ responded.

The Chief turned to one of the other officers at the scene and told him to get a broadcast out at once.

Rich Bentley turned and walked over to the now covered body of his good friend, Ed Castillo. He knelt down and gently touched Castillo's shoulder. He paused for almost thirty seconds, and then stood up and proclaimed in a loud voice, "Find me the bustard who did this!"

JJ was still shaken by the murder of his former fellow police officer. The news reporter was trying desperately to get close enough to him to blurt out yet another stupid question, but the reporter was kept at bay.

14

JoJo, as the bangers called him, was just under five feet tall. He got his nick name from the other bangers because he reminded them of an organ grinder's monkey. He was offended at first, but he had more than proved his worth to the Latin Lords now.

The wiry little JoJo was often mistaken for a grade schooler with a cigarette dangling out of his mouth. Local officers found him amusing and often made fun of him themselves, *a little banger trying to look bad,* they would think.

JoJo pedaled his bike down several narrow alleys and then hid behind an abandon house until the chaos slowed down. His heart was beating fast and he was excited. He was going to collect the reward for killing the cop that offed Eddy's younger brother. This was already his second kill, now they had to recognize him as a macho banger for sure. He couldn't wait to get back to the clubhouse and let Eddy, and everyone else, know it was him that pulled the trigger. He offed the pig who killed Eddy's brother.

With visions of the one-thousand-dollar bounty that Eddy had put on that JJ's head, JoJo was already spending the money.

I'm going to get me a bad ass ride man. Cooler than any ride in the club. Even Eddy will be jealous of my ride. It will be low and slow and sound real mean.

JoJo sat behind the dilapidated old house three blocks away from the crime scene, listening to the sirens as he puffed on a reefer and smiled to himself.

Maybe I will be the jefe of the Lords one of these days. Yah, that's it. Then they will have to give me a new name, a name with respect, not this JoJo shit.

Darkness had finally fallen on the little old neighborhood and JoJo ditched the bicycle in the bushes and headed back to the clubhouse on foot. He couldn't wait to get there. He was sure the place would already be bustling with the news.

JoJo approached the clubhouse but he didn't see any of the familiar rides that were normally parked out front. He was hoping for a grand entrance but, as long as Eddy was there, that's all that mattered for now. The rest of the club would know soon enough what he had done for Eddy. He was the man.

"You stupid little bastard, what have you done?" Eddy blurted out as JoJo entered through the front door.

"What do you mean bro, I just killed the pig that killed your brother! You owe me a thousand dollars!"

"Idiot, you offed the wrong pig!"

"You killed Castillo, the head of the gang unit. We will not be safe in this town ever again. You have screwed us bad JoJo!"

"But..."

"You need to get out of town now. If you are still here in fifteen minutes, I will turn you over to the pigs myself."

"But Jefe, I don't have any way to travel, all I have is a two-wheeler."

"Get on you bicycle and start pedaling your skinny ass out of town. If the cops don't get you, the Latin Lords will, and I promise you JoJo, you will be better off if the cops get you first. Now get the hell out of here and never show your face in this town again!"

JoJo didn't know what to say. He went from total excitement to total failure in just minutes. His one true hero had just banned him from his club and his town.

15

"For Christ sake Eddy I'm only fifteen. Where do you think I could go without a ride or money? I live with my parents and I wouldn't have a place to stay if I left here," JoJo said with his hands on his hips.

I don't give a shit, punk. Just get your ass out of here and never come back!"

Eddy turned and started to walk away when JoJo screamed at him,

"You were my hero Eddy, but now you call me punk."

Eddy turned back to face JoJo and was looking down the barrel of JoJo's gun. Eddy wasn't armed because one of the rules was never bring a firearm into the clubhouse in case they were raided during a meeting. But now JoJo had made another mistake and stood there with his gun pointed at Eddy's head. The kid started shaking.

"You ain't got the guts to shoot me, you little piss ant."

"I shot the cop, didn't I?" JoJo said changing his aim to Eddy's heart. The longer they stood there, the more the kid shook. Eddy took a few steps toward JoJo and the kid squeezed the trigger. The bullet hit Eddy in the shoulder sending him backwards into a pile of chairs. Eddy put his hand over the wound in an effort to stop the bleeding.

"Give me your car keys and your money," JoJo said with tears in his eyes. Eddy knew if he resisted JoJo would shoot him again, so he tossed his keys and a a roll of bills at JoJo.

Eddy's car was parked in the rear of the clubhouse. He managed to get to his feet and staggered out the front door and started to cross the street when he fainted.

. A motorist stopped and called 911 and soon Eddy was on his way to the hospital. The word that Eddy had been shot spread quickly through the neighborhood. Rumors were flying but most of them were saying the cops did it for revenge of Castillo's hit. A war was forming up between the Latin Lords and Bakersfield PD.

Eddy lay in his hospital bed waiting for his scheduled surgery to remove the bullet. He lost about a pint of blood before he arrived at the hospital. This wasn't the first time Eddy had been shot. Once in the stomach and another time in the leg. He wore the scars like a badge of honor.

Sergeant Mike Keel who was second in charge of the gang unit appeared at Eddy's open door and knocked lightly. Eddy had met Sergeant Keel a few times before and waved him in.

"Hey Eddy how you feeling?" Keel asked.

"Fuck man, how do you think I feel? Like I've been shot!"

"Sorry man that was a dumb question."

"Yeah, and maybe I'll tell everyone a cop shot me for no reason," Eddy said in anger.

"Yeah, like that will fly," Keel answered.

Eddy didn't want to tell the cops it was JoJo. He wanted the Latin Lords to find the kid and keep him hidden until he was well enough to kill JoJo himself. Eddy turned his head away from Sergeant Keel and refused to talk anymore.

"I'll be back tomorrow," Keel said as he walked out of Eddy's room.

Eddy could hear his cell phone ringing. It was in his pants hanging in the hospital room closet. He slowly made his way to the closet and pulled his phone from the pants pocket. The display showed it was from Jose, one of his lieutenants. Eddy spoke quietly and told Jose who had shot him and that the kid had taken Eddy's ride. Then he went on to explain what he wanted them to do in regard to the kid.

"We will take care of it Boss," they hung up.

The hospital staff came in and prepared to take Eddy to surgery. One of the nurses gave him a shot causing him to drift into lala land.

16

JJ's cell phone rang, the display showed it was from Turrie.

"I'm glad you called sweetheart. I know you were planning on visiting me this weekend but right now that would not be a good idea."

He went on to tell her everything that had happened and that he was moving his parents out of their home to a safer location.

"I'd love to see you but if you were here I would always be in fear for your life. The whole city is in a state of panic."

"Call me every day honey, I need to know that you are alright," Turrie demanded.

"10-4 sweetie," JJ hung up.

~ ~ ~

JoJo headed to the small town of Taft, California where he had a cousin named Lester Morales who was his same age. He stopped for gas and got directions to Taft. It had been several years ago when he and his parents had visited Taft for a family reunion.

JoJo remembered his cousin's home was on a hill that overlooked the city. He was sure he could find their house. When he arrived in Taft, there was only one hill of any size and he didn't have any trouble finding their place. Lester was outside working on his Chevy Impala, as JoJo pulled up.

"Sweet ride," Lester hollered as he waved to JoJo.

"Hey Lester, I need a place to stay for a while, can you help me out? I've got some problems with the Latin Lords."

"Come on in and have a beer. You can tell me all about what happened." Lester answered, thinking JoJo still looked like a little kid.

For the next hour, they drank and JoJo told Lester the whole story.

"Man, you got some serious shit ahead of you," Lester said.

"Think your folks will let me hole up here for a few days?"

"Yeah, no problem they're at work now and I don't expect them home until 9:00 pm. You can share my room."

"I didn't bring anything with we, left in a big hurry you know." They talked for another hour.

"Those beers made me sleepy, would you mind if I caught an hour or so of sleep?"

"Na, go for it cousin, I'll finish what I was doing on my car and catch you later."

As Lester was finishing replacing his old battery with a new one, he began to think. *I don't need any trouble with the Latin Lords and neither does my folks. If they find out JoJo is hiding at our place they'll make us pay with our lives.* Lester drove to a banger house he knew and asked how to get in touch with the Latin Lords.

"What's it concern?" the banger asked.

"They're looking for a guy and I know where he is hiding."

The banger dialed a number on his cell phone and handed it to Lester.

A gruff voice answered.

"What you want?"

"My name is Lester Morales and I live in Taft California. I understand you are looking for JoJo and I know where he is hiding. I don't want trouble with the Lords so that's why I'm calling you. He's my cousin and he just showed up at our house and told me what he had done."

"Give me your address," the voice said.

"Promise me that my family and I won't be harmed."

"You are doing us a solid and we will owe you in the future," the voice answered.

"261 Hill St." Lester said.

"Gracias Amigo," the phone went dead.

~ ~ ~

The cops were sure that one of the Latin Lords shot Ed Castillo but they didn't know which one pulled the trigger. Everyone on the gang detail knew their job had just gotten a lot harder. It would be up to them to flush out the shooter and make the bangers pay for Castillo's murderer.

The Chief had assigned Sergeant Mike Keel to head up the gang unit. Keel was known to the rest of the BPD as Crazy Mike. He had been a Marine Corps sniper in Viet Nam, and was credited with over one hundred kills.

Sergeant Bentley met with Keel at a donut shop on the north side of town. They were sure they could talk freely at that location.

Keel looked around, and the shop was empty. The owner brought them each a coffee and a donut.

"On the house," he said and walked away. The owner was always happy to have the cops stop by and spend a little time. Donut shops and convenient stores are always an easy target for stop and robs.

Sergeant Bentley began, "I know who pulled the trigger, and where he is hiding. I'm not giving up my CI, so don't ask. The shooter has been resting quietly at a location in Taft. It's a kid named JoJo. You can guess what the Latin Lord's will be planning."

Keel was stunned.

"John, are you going to the Chief with this?"

"I don't know. I have several options. The Chief is one. There are a few others." His voice took on a strange tone. It was not a pleasant tone. "Ed Castillo was a friend who went back to our time in the jungle. Not many people know, but Ed and I were a team in the Central Highlands of Viet Nam. He saved my butt more than once. I couldn't save him this time and it hurts."

Sergeant Bentley nodded. "I think I understand, but Castillo would not have wanted you to go down in flames and lose everything over some banger. You and your family would suffer greatly. I'm sure Ed would have wanted you to do this the right way."

Keel hesitated for a moment, "Yeah, Ed would have wanted it done the right way. He was like that. Let's go to the Chief and lay this shit on him."

They went directly to see the Chief. Sergeant Keel described his conversation with his source, and suggested bringing in both Kern County Sheriff's and Taft Police to handle the JoJo issue. Although they would be outside their jurisdiction when in Taft, they wanted to be in on the action. The Chief agreed, and called the Kern County Sheriff on his personal line. They discussed the situation, and agreed to have a conference call with the Chief over at Taft. While the brass talked, Sergeant Keel contacted the BPD Air Unit. At the moment, they had two, four passenger helicopters available. The Kern County Sheriff Air Unit had an additional two helicopters capable of carrying four passengers.

The Sheriff and the two Chiefs agreed to cooperate with the apprehension of the banger named JoJo. They also agreed that time was critical. Taft PD had sent an unmarked unit to the address where the banger was hiding. Taft PD would use one of their officers in civilian clothes driving an old city truck for site surveillance. Kern County had two marked units and an unmarked unit available for the operation. Sergeants Keel and

Bentley would go by helicopter to Taft where they would meet Taft PD and KCSO at the West Side Hospital helipad. The Brass decided that Taft PD would be the lead organization since it was their jurisdiction. Sergeants Keel and Bentley would take an active role under the Mutual Aid Pact for Kern County. The DA had already agreed to the legal aspects of the plan, and had his Chief Deputy coming in front of a friendly Kern County Judge for an arrest warrant on JoJo.

Thirty minutes later, Keel and Bentley were airborne in a helicopter on their way to Taft. KCSO and Taft PD units were waiting at the hospital, and the Taft PD surveillance truck was driving by the target location. The surveillance officer described a vehicle parked at the side of the property. A phone call to the BPD Gang Unit confirmed the description of the vehicle was the same as one driven by Eddy Gallegos. The vehicle description confirmed the details given to Keel by his source. JoJo was definitely at this location.

17

The black, four door SUV with heavily tinted windows, was driving toward Taft on Highway 119. The three Latin Lords listened to a Mexican music radio station as they drove the speed limit. They seldom left their home turf. But today, they were on a mission, a deadly mission. The little asshole, JoJo, had put their gang in jeopardy. He tried to be a banger, but was nothing but a loser. He killed once before, but it was a young girl, not a banger. The girl had become a problem. She was talking to the cops, and that was bad for the Latin Lord's business.

Their plan was to go to the house where JoJo was staying and grab him and take Eddy's ride, then head back to the clubhouse. At least the car would make it back to the clubhouse. JoJo would make it to a field or a ditch somewhere in the Valley. They would take him down at the house. If he tried to fight, they would end it there, but if they could take him without a fight, he would ride in the trunk wearing duct tape on his hands behind his back and a wide strip across his mouth.

California Highway Patrol Officer Dennis Bailey sat in his cruiser on the edge of highway 119 facing northbound from the city of Taft. A blacked out SUV with heavily tinted windows passed him. His radar readout indicated the driver was traveling five miles an hour under the speed limit. The window tint and the lower than posted speed limit caused something in him to take pause. He could understand a local pickup or sedan going below the limit, but not that type of vehicle. The CHP cruiser accelerated to catch the SUV. About two miles north of Taft, the CHP Officer lit up the car and ordered it to pull over. The SUV was still traveling below the speed limit, but it did not pull over to the shoulder. The driver continued until it came to an intersection with a dirt road seldom used by regular traffic, where the driver pulled to a stop about two hundred feet from the highway. At first CHP Officer Bailey didn't know what was happening. His cop sense started sending danger signals. He stopped his unit about fifty feet behind the SUV and called in the vehicles description and plate number. He had stopped far enough away to keep his options open. Soon dispatch notified him the vehicle came back clean.

The driver of the SUV was sweating. The gang member setting in the passenger seat was a new member of the Latin Lords that the driver disliked, because he had made unwanted advances toward his sister. Each of the occupants were armed, and the gang was already in heavy trouble because JoJo had offed a cop. Now here they were, confronted with a bad situation. The two passengers in the back seat were more nervous than the driver, and looked to him for help.

Everything is screwed up since yesterday. A dead cop back in the hood, and now this because of that dumb jerk JoJo. The driver sat there, trying to come up with a solution. They could fight or run. Then the driver came up with an idea. He turned and looked at the new member in the front seat.

"Open your door!" the driver said.

The passenger looked at the driver with wide eyes. "What?"

"Open the door!" The driver shouted.

"Are you serious?" the new member asked with a real look of concern creeping across his face.

"Yes, God damn it. Open the fucking door!"

The passenger looked at the driver. The driver had his Glock pointed at the passenger. "Open the damned door now, asshole!" the driver demanded.

The passenger saw the rage in the driver's eyes and complied.

As soon as the door opened, and the new gang member stepped out, he took a 40 caliber bullet in the head. He was dead before he hit the ground. The driver stepped on the gas causing the passengers door to swing shut all by its self, and sped away in a cloud of dust. The back-seat passengers sat with their eyes wide still trying to understand what had just happened.

Officer Bailey could not believe what he just saw happened.

"That should keep the cops busy while we get our asses out of here. Now, let's go get the little bastard JoJo," the driver said.

18

The CHP officer ran over to check on the gunshot victim, while the black SUV continued down the farm road until they found a cross road where they could double back toward the highway and leave the dust behind them..

The CHP Officer stood over the banger's body that was left in the roadway.

He tracked the progress of the SUV by the dust cloud the car caused in its wake. Backup was on the way. The CHP Officer chose to stay at the crime scene and let responding units pick up the chase. It was not long before two units pulled up at the officer's location.

"Follow that dust trail, they're the ones that shot this guy." The two units sped off after he had given them a brief story of the shooting and a description of the SUV.

CHP Officers were used to working the highways, and their units were designed for high speed chases on smooth surfaces, not a bumping along on dirt roads designed for farm vehicles. The black SUV remained out in front of the pursuing officers who were slow to close the gap between the hunted and the hunters. As the chase continued, the officers were gaining on the suspects but were still out of visual contact and were relying on the dust cloud for their bearings.

Soon the officers began to close in on the dust cloud and although they could not see the vehicle because of the thick dust in the air, they knew they were getting closer to the SUV.

Suddenly the officer in the lead car slammed on his brakes and fishtailed in the soft dirt coming to rest a few feet short of a large tractor. The second car also slid to a stop just missing his fellow officer's vehicle. As the dust cloud rolled past and the scene in front of them became visible the officers realized the suspects were gone and their path on the dirt road was blocked by an oversized tractor and a very bewildered farm hand. They looked ahead but could no longer see the bangers vehicle or it's tell tail dust trail.

"Shit," the first officer said. "Get on the radio and let everyone know we lost them."

The second officer returned to his vehicle to put out a broadcast while the first officer spoke to the tractor driver.

"You've taken up the whole road with your tractor, how did they get past you?" The first officer asked the tractor driver.

"No habla English," the driver responded.

Having worked the Central Valley long enough to know that the tractor driver was not going to get involved in a matter between the police and some gang banger types, the officer simply nodded and returned to his vehicle.

"Any luck with the tractor driver?" The second officer asked when his beat partner returned.

"He doesn't want to get involved," The officer said.

"Did he say that?" the second officer asked.

"No, not exactly. He gave me the no habla English routine so I didn't push it."

"I speak Spanish, want me to talk to him?" The second officer asked.

"No, I don't want to put him in the middle of this, just go ask him to pull his tractor over so we can get by and we will follow the road to see where it leads. While you're doing that I will let communications know what we plan to do."

After the tractor moved to the side, the officers followed the dirt road until it intersected with the main highway. They turned and headed back to the shooting scene. By the time they got to the scene the place looked like the parking lot of a Dodger game. There were several police units from various agencies and a couple of ambulances. The officers parked and walked over to what appeared to be a makeshift command center, a torn and tattered county map spread over the hood of a black and white. They could see their lieutenant was studying the map intently. The lieutenant looked up. "What happened out there?" The lieutenant asked.

"They were able to leave us stranded behind a farm tractor. By the time we got around it and back on the trail they had made it to the highway and were out of sight." The first officer said.

"Any idea where they went?" The Lieutenant asked.

"I assumed they got to the highway, and probably headed north. Otherwise someone would have spotted them as they passed by here. There are enough cops around that they couldn't all be sleeping."

"Any ideas about what their next move might be? Think on that a minute," the Lieutenant said to the group assembled around the map. He stepped away to answer his cell phone that he had attached to his belt.

"We have no idea who they are or why they are in these parts so it could be anything," one of the officers said.

"Well, maybe I do," the Lieutenant said as he walked back to the group. "That call was from Bakersfield PD. They had an officer killed earlier and they have traced the suspect to a house in Taft. They have a unit watching the place and a tactical team on the way."

"What's that have to do with our case?" someone asked.

"Well it seems that the punk who killed the officer also shot the main man in the Latin Lords' gang. He then fled in the El Jefe prized ride and rumor on the street is, the gang placed a price on the shooter's head and sent people out to find him and bring him back for a meeting with the wounded boss."

"He better hope the police get to him first, cause I'm guessing that going to jail, even with the murder of a police officer on his head, is a lot better option than letting the gang take him alive."

"Suicide by cop would be his best option," one of the officers said, followed by mumbled agreement from the rest of the group.

"Well, that's someone else's problem for now. Let's get back to finding our murder suspects," the Lieutenant said.

"My gut tells me they have switched cars by now, so most likely we need to be ready to follow up on any stolen vehicle reports," an officer said.

"I agree," the Lieutenant said. "So let's do this. Hansen, you and Helms are still assigned as back-up on the shooting so why don't you keep with that, at least for now. I'll put you out on a special detail. Does that work?"

Hansen looks at Helms who nodded, then Hansen said, "Works for us. What do you want us to do?"

"I'm thinking you guys head to where you think our suspects came back onto the highway. Slowly cruise north and hope we get lucky. Either of you spot the missing SUV or you hear about a stolen vehicle, let me know. I'll have at least one unit from the north sector do a southbound search and you guys can meet half way."

"You got it boss," the two officers said as they turned and headed to their cars.

"Don't get too far apart and don't approach anyone without back-up. These are bad people and we don't need any other men getting shot," the lieutenant called after them.

The officers search about 10 miles north without any luck. They met a southbound unit who also had come up empty. The two officers talked for a few minutes then split up and headed back the way they came. Hansen and Helms decided to take the frontage road instead of the highway and planned to check all the yards and roads on the way back. After leapfrogging each other and driving in and out of back roads and driveways the two units were within a couple of miles of the shooting when Hansen spotted a car parked back in the trees next to an irrigation canal. It was the same color as the SUV so Hansen radioed for backup then parked, blocking the road and waited for Helms. When Helms arrived the two officers approached the vehicle. It was the missing SUV. The officers checked the car. It was empty but they hear singing and splashing coming from the irrigation canal. There was a naked man splashing around in the canal. They walked a hundred feet to where the canal went under the road.

"You in the water, don't move!" Hansen ordered.

The man looked up to see the officers pointing their guns at him and he yelled, "Don't shoot. I'm not hurting anyone. I'll leave right now."

"Why don't you come out of the water so we can talk." Hansen said.

The man waded over to the side of the ditch and began to climb out, dropping a whiskey bottle in the process.

"Shit," the naked man said as he reached down for the bottle without thinking.

"Freeze," Hansen said.

The man stood up straight, put his hands in the air, and froze like a marble statue.

"That was close partner. I almost shot a naked man." Helms said.

The officers got the man out of the water and sat him on the bank. "Where are your clothes?" Helms asked.

"Over there hanging on the bushes," the man answered.

Helms went over to where the man's pants were and searched the pockets before handing them to the man. After he man put them on Helms put him in handcuffs. When the situation was secured the officers got the man's story. Seems he was washing up in the water when three Mexican guys drove up in the car. They give him the keys and the whiskey and told him the car was his.

"There did they go?" Hansen asked.

"They took my car and left me there. They all got in and drove off."

"Describe your car to us"

"Oh.., she old and beat up," the farm hand said.

"Come on amigo explain more about your car." Hanson said.

"Okay, it's a Ford and she is green automatic."

"What year?"

"I not know." He answered.

"Are you the owner?"

"No, I find car parked in field. It been there a long time. I got it to run again and used it for the farm. The farm hand said in broken English.

"Did you see where they went?" Helms asked.

"No, they told me not to look, so I shut my eyes and put my head down. Those are the kind of men you don't mess with."

"Anything else?" Hansen asked.

"I forgot about the gun."

"Gun, what gun?" Hansen asked.

"Well, all of them have guns. I could tell that. But the man who talked, was the boss man I guess, he had this gun pointed at me while they were here. When they were getting ready to leave he tossed it in the water and told me it was mine if I could find it."

"Get hold of the Lieutenant and have him get some people out here to search the canal for the gun and take possession of our friend and his new SUV." Helms told Hanson.

19

The little gangster JoJo felt pretty safe at the moment. He was kicked back on the ratty old flee infested couch at Lester's, eating Cheetos and watching 'I Love Lucy' reruns on television. *No one knows about my cousin's place here in Taft for sure man. When this blows over, I will figure something out.* He patted the 9MM stolen pistol in his waistband for confidence. *I will start my own gang. I will be the El Jefe and no one can tell me what to do. I will call my gang 'Barrio Kings'. We will take over the hood. The Latin Lords will fear us more than anything, man!*

~ ~ ~

Sergeant Bentley's cell phone rang. "Bentley here." he responded.

"We just got an update from the CHP regarding their shooting on Highway 119 just south of here. They are sure it was a carload of bangers and they are most likely coming after your suspect as we speak." The dispatcher operator said.

"Anything further?" Bentley asked.

"Only that the occupants of the SUV apparently dumped their car and picked up an old beat up station wagon from a farm worker who was irrigating a field about five miles from the CHP crime scene."

"Okay, do you have a description of the station wagon for us?" Bentley asked.

"Only that it is an old Ford, year unknown. It was reported to be light green in color and pretty beat up," the dispatcher answered.

"Thanks," Bentley said as he hung up the phone.

"Sergeant Keel, notify the air units to be on the lookout for that green station wagon. We don't need them crashing our surveillance scene before we take our suspect down. Also make sure all of our ground units from Taft and Kern County have the information as well. This could turn into an all-out gang war with the law if we are not careful."

~ ~ ~

The most important thing on JJ's mind right now was getting his parents safely over to Ojai. The moving van had just pulled away from the old family home in Bakersfield where his family had spent the biggest share of their lives. It was a bittersweet event to say the least. JJ took one last look around and then got in the car and left the house for good. Now the house would belong to the Diocese of Bakersfield to do with what they choose.

JJ had been able to secure a storage unit large enough for their belongings and what was left of his father's tools.

As time permits, they can sort through things together and decide what to keep and what to get rid of, he thought.

Turrie had helped find a small apartment for JJ's parents to live in while they looked for an acceptable retirement home. She was very excited to have JJ back in Ojai so they could resume their relationship where it had left off weeks before.

JJ's first order of business, now that he was back in Ojai, was to meet with Chief Olson and present him with a work release document from his doctor. JJ was so excited he could hardly wait to hand it to the Chief.

"Hey Chief, it's me, your favorite wounded duck reporting back to duty," JJ said with a big smile.

Everyone in the station applauded; all three of them.

"No one is happier than us to have you back Officer Nolan. The town of Ojai will be safe once more!" the Chief laughed. "Seriously JJ, we are pleased and honored to have you back in one piece. I am going to put you on the day shift for awhile so you can get back in the groove and help your parents get settled in."

"Thanks Chief, I appreciate everything you have done for both Turrie and I. Have you received any further information from Bakersfield on what's going on with the Latin Lords gang?"

"Not as of this morning, I do know they have a lead on the shooter and have formed a task-force with Taft PD and Kern County SO to go after him, but that's it so far. I will keep you posted if I hear anything more."

"Thanks Chief."

As he left the station, JJ thought about Sergeant Castillo and the poor Delgado girl. *This has to stop before any more people or officers get hurt. We have to squash the Latin Lords.*

~ ~ ~

JoJo pulled out his cell phone as he finished up the bag of Cheetos and tried to reach Lester again.

Where is that essay, why is he not around here? We need to get some Dos Equis or some Corona Carver in this place man. How can he expect me to stay here if we don't have supplies?

JoJo got up off the couch to take a pee. He was getting bored and restless. He thought about taking Eddy's car for a little ride around Taft, but then thought better of it. No one here knew him, but they would surely remember the car if anyone was asking around.

Come dark, I need to get out and get some air, he told himself as he settled back down on the couch for another TV rerun.

JoJo found himself increasingly unable to hear the television because of some loud noise outside. A helicopter or something was causing a harshness sound. *The bastards,* he thought as he turned the television louder. Then he turned it up again. Finally JoJo threw the remote on the floor and got up to find out what was making all the noise.

It was not one helicopter, but two. And they were straight above the house.

Fucking Lester sold me out man! I gotta get out of here! JoJo grabbed the car keys to Eddy's ride and opened the front door. He pulled the 9MM from his pants and racked a round into the chamber.

What JoJo saw next all but made him pee his pants. There were no less that ten cars surrounding the property. Some were marked patrol cars and others were plain looking vehicles. But they all had cops behind them. He quickly slammed the door and ran to the back of the house and looked through the bathroom window. They were there as well. *What now?*

He grabbed his cell phone and dialed Lester's number one last time. There was no answer.

Rot in hell Lester, you asshole!

JoJo went back to the front door and opened it just a crack. As he did, the loud speaker on top of one of the squad cars sprang to life and called him by name, telling him to step out with both of his hands in the air.

"No way you cops are going to take me alive," he shouted back over the noise of the two helicopters. Eddy's car was only fifteen feet from the house.

If I can make it that far, I can bust through and make a run for it. A thought typical of JoJo's 15 year old irrational mentality.

Seconds later, he fired three shots randomly in the direction of the officers, causing them all to scatter and duck for cover. He took off running toward the car. When reaching it, he firmly grabbed the door handle and pulled. It didn't open. He jerked as hard as he could, but the door still would not open. It had been locked by one of the cops. "Fuck you Lester!" he screamed at the top of his lungs as he turned toward the officers and fired again.

From the little farm road, a quarter of a mile away, the dirty old Ford station wagon sat and watched the rest of the event unfold. It was only a matter of ten or fifteen seconds and it was all over.

"Essay, let's get the Hell out of here. We don't need any of that shit coming down on us.. They must have shot him a hundred times. Let's go, come on let's go!" They were right JoJo had been shot multiple times. When the body was examined by the coroner the exact amount of wounds would be reported.

The beat up old station wagon turned and headed in the opposite direction back toward the clubhouse. They didn't know what would be worse, telling Eddy the Cops got JoJo, or telling Eddy that the cops totally destroyed his prize ride with bullets.

20

Although it was a totally different car, it reminded everyone of the famous photographs of Bonny and Clyde's bullet ridden automobile when the police had trapped them and the famous duo was killed.

Most of the cops on scene had their cell phones out and were taking pictures. Someone at the scene sent a picture to a Bakersfield local newspaper in hopes of pissing off Eddy Gallegos even more. They were standing around Eddy's ride taking pictures of each other in front of the demolished car when Taft's Police Chief intervened.

"Knock that shit off right now before the press gets here and posts a picture of you idiots standing around the car like a bunch of meat-heads gloating over an over kill. I want each of you to canvas the nearby homes to see if everyone is okay and that no stray bullets has caused the residents any damage or God forbid injuries." He had barely got the words out of his mouth when the press arrived.

They cornered Taft's Police Chief and the questions began. His response was, "No comment," but that didn't stop the news hungry reporters from continuing pestering the Chief.

Soon a tow truck arrived. The driver hooked up Eddy's car and towed it away. Down the street a cop had stopped a young man driving a 1965 partially restored Chevy Impala.

"What's your business here?" the cop asked.

My name is Lester Morales and that's my house where all the cop cars are."

"Let's see your drivers license," the cop demanded.

Lester had it tucked above his visor. He reached up slowly to retrieve it and handed it to the officer.

"Okay kid, go ahead but drive slow and don't make any suspicious moves. Those cops down there are on edge," the officer said pointing in the direction of all the assembled law enforcement vehicles.

Lester stopped in front of his house and noticed JoJo's ride was gone and then he saw a white sheet with blood spots covering what appeared to be a body. He got out of his car and asked the nearest cop who was under the sheet.

"A little skinny kid who decided to have a gun battle with us rather than give up. He must have been brain dead to think he could beat the odds of twenty-five to one."

It had been fifteen minutes from the time of the shooting when the County Coroner's wagon rolled up to the house. They lifted the white sheet and shook their heads. One was heard to say, "What a mess, and the kid looks so young." They went about their business. When finished they placed young JoJo's corpse in a body bag and transported him to the morgue.

Taft's Police Chief thanked everyone involved and each of the various agencies before they left for their home turf. It was nice to see the cooperation between all the departments.

The news that a young Hispanic male had shot it out with the cops in Taft spread through the community like a wild brush-fire on a windy day.

Lester was saddened that he had caused his cousin's death but he was not going to tell his parents what he did. He had stayed clear of the gangs for the most part. They didn't seem to be that well organized in Taft.

Not only did the shootout make the news in Bakersfield, there was a large article in the Los Angeles Times that even showed Eddy's car. Evidently someone had told the reporter about the extensive amount of bullet holes in the vehicle. The reporter found out where the tow truck had taken the car and went to that location to get pictures to go along with the news story.

It took a lot of heat away from the Latin Lords and put it on the cops for the killing of a fifteen year-old youth as a payback for the murder of Sergeant Castillo. The news article didn't mention officer Castillo's murder.

~ ~ ~

Turrie was working graveyard shift and JJ was working the day shift. It put a strain on their relationship especially with different days off. She would be coming home just as he would be leaving for work. JJ knew it wouldn't be that long before he could switch to the graveyard shift and things would be all right again. He also knew that Eddy would no doubt up the ante for the person that took him out.

Ojai was a relatively small city with two large beats to cover. That meant back-up could be a long way off if someone needed help in a hurry. He also knew the way Eddy would play it. JJ was betting Eddy would create a bogus call in the other beat, then try to ambush him when he least expected it and no backup would be available.

JJ was right, that was exactly what Eddy was planning, but he wanted to wait until the heat had gone down before he put his plan into action. He also wanted time for JJ to relax while on duty.

After his shift JJ took the Delgado file and drove to where Lisa Delgado's body was found and walked the area in hopes of uncovering a new piece of evidence linking her murder to the Latin Lords. He was unable to locate anything. He opened the file and made note of the name and address of the female hiker who had discovered Lisa Delgado. He decided to pay her a visit.

JJ arrived at the address listed on the file, parked and walked up to the house and knocked on the front door. A thin young woman with dark hair opened the door and stood there in silence.

"I'm JJ Nolan from the Ojai police department. Are you Melanie Shuts?" he asked.

"Yes, how can I help you Officer Nolan?"

"The other day when you discovered the woman's body while hiking did you find any other items close by?"

Melanie was shocked by the question and was slow to answer.

"Why do you ask..?" she finally said with her hands clasped together in front of her.

"Well, her mother told us Lisa's body was missing her favorite ring," JJ said.

Melanie quickly looked down at her hands and then looked up at JJ.

"Yes, I took it. I didn't think she'd need it anymore. I also found a man's watch nearby. Am I in big trouble?" she asked.

"Not that serious, I'm sure. Do you still have those items?" JJ asked.

"Yes sir I do." She slipped a pretty white gold and pearl ring off her finger, and handed it to JJ.

"What about the man's watch?"

"It's inside. I'll get it for you." She said in a weak trembling voice.

This would be a pile of paperwork but it could possibly be a lead to Ms. Delgado's killer, JJ thought.

Melanie returned to the doorway with a plastic bag containing a man's gold watch. JJ could see an inscription on its back. It read, "To Teddy from Lisa 1999."

He thanked Ms. Shuts and told her someone from the department would be in touch with her. When he returned to the OPD headquarters he dusted the items for prints. None were visible. Nolan called Sergeant Bentley and told him about the watch and ring.

"How did you know a ring was missing?"

"Dumb luck I guess. She kept holding her hands like she was trying to hide something. I just got a glimpse of a ring and thought that was it."

"Did her mother ever say there was a ring missing?" Bentley asked.

"Na, I never talked with Lisa's mother," JJ responded.

"I'll call the gang unit and see if they are aware of a banger in the Lords by the name of Teddy. If there is they can work him into believing there was a print on the back of his watch that was found near Lisa Delgado's body. That should scare the crap out of him," Bentley said.

~ ~ ~

Officer Nolan cruised slowly through the quiet neighborhoods and the businesses that made Ojai the tranquil place depicted by the Chamber of Commerce. A sleepy little village where everyone was safe. JJ knew better. He was listening and watching for any unusual activity or people. He was certain that the Latin Lords would be coming, so he made extra passes by his parents and his girlfriend's place. He cared more for them than for himself.

The sun had set and the Bakersfield residents were turning on their house lights. It was almost dark and streets were quiet. The city was still in the grips of temperatures in the high 90's.

Bakersfield metro area had nearly 350,000 people, it was a rural town and it seemed as though the sidewalks automatically rolled up at sunset. The ranch hands and cowboys were changing into their social duds and heading out to the dance halls, or beer bars for the evening of drinking, dancing, or fights, or which ever you liked the best. The white collar working people and the office workers were getting ready for sleep in order to be rested for tomorrows work day.

But not Eddy. Eddy was alert and pissed. His prized possession, his decked out ride, was gone. Several members of his gang were gone. The cops had painted a bulls-eye on his back because of a little jerk named JoJo. Now there was another murder outside Taft that might be tied to his gang.

No, Eddy was not sleeping the peaceful sleep.

Maybe I should go down to Altadena, California and stay with my cousins for a while, he thought. His cell phone rang. Teddy was calling him in the middle of the night. What the hell was going on?

"Boss, boss, you there?" Teddy was either high or drunk.

Eddy immediately hung up. He did not want to talk to Teddy right now, especially on the phone. Maybe the cops were listening. He knew the gang was getting a lot of heat. The Latin Lords were accused of killing a Bakersfield cop, shooting an Ojai cop and getting into a shootout in Taft. He did not need any more problems, but he also was forced to come up with a solution for the many immediate problems facing the gang. He needed time to think. He wanted to leave the city, but JoJo and the cops had destroyed his ride. He looked forward to getting even with that Ojai cop. Maybe sooner than later.

~ ~ ~

Sergeant Keel was working too many hours. He tried to go home for some sleep, but he could not get any rest. His brain would not stop working. He was unconscious in his bedroom for two hours. It was not sleep, it was exhaustion. He woke with a start, looked at the clock, and decided to go back to the office. He intended to destroy the Latin Lords. They had gone too far. They had made it personal.

The Patrol Shift Commander met Keel in the hallway outside the gang unit. "What are you doing here? It's the middle of the night."

Keel looked at him and said, "Can't sleep. This Latin Lords thing is killing me. Maybe if I review enough intel and field reports, I can find something useful."

The Shift Commandeer nodded. "If you need anything give me a call."

Keel sat at his desk. Ed Castillo's desk was clean and unused, but Keel avoided the small office. He opened a liter bottle of Pepsi and went to work at his desk. He was reading the report from the JoJo incident when the Shift Commander came into the room.

"I was reviewing the reports from the evening shift when I came across this field report reporting a car fire behind an abandoned strip mall out in the southwest district. Bakersfield Fire responded and found the vehicle fully involved. They extinguished the fire with little damage to the buildings, but the car was a mess. When it cooled, they towed the remains to a salvage yard. The yard sent the VIN to us and we ran it. The vehicle was a fifteen-year old Ford station wagon registered to a rural address out near Taft. CHP had a murder and stolen car incident out near Taft at about the same time of the Latin Lords shootout. It might be a stretch, but maybe this station wagon is connected to the CHP murder and the Latin Lords."

Keel looked up from his papers, "I guess somebody will be available at CHP in a few hours. I'll give them a call. Maybe these incidents are connected. Thanks," Keel offered.

The Shift Commander looked directly at Keel. "I liked Ed, too." He walked back out into the hallway, and Keel was left alone with his thoughts.

Keel pulled out a stack of three by five cards and began to write a piece of data on each card. That made him feel like he was making progress even if he was just wasting time. He was organizing facts as he knew them. Possibly, he would find a pattern or connections between people, places and incidents.

What did he have so far?

Officer Nolan shooting in Ojai.

Bakersfield girl with Latin Lords connections shot and killed in Ojai.

Latin Lords shooting of BPD Sergeant Castillo in Bakersfield.

Probable target was Ojai Officer Nolan.

Harassment of Officer Nolan's parents in Bakersfield.

Shoot out in Taft resulting in death of Latin Lord shooter of Sergeant Castillo.

Shooting death of young Mexican male outside Taft near the time of the JoJo shootout.

The sun was about to spring over the top of the Sierras, but Keel would not see the fiery red ball. With arms folded and head on his desk, he fell asleep.

21

Officer JJ Nolan was back on patrol in the sleepy little city of Ojai. His workload was the usual mixture of business disputes, traffic problems and tourist questions. In the back of his mind Nolan could not shake the feeling that danger still lurked waiting for the chance to invade his tranquil world. The day shift was not JJ's cup of tea and he would much prefer to go back to late nights so in part he didn't have to deal with the petty problems he encountered during the day, but mostly because he could spend more time with his girlfriend. With this shift the two were like ships passing in the night. One off to bed while the other was off to work.

Day shift did give JJ his evenings free but between trying to squeeze in a couple of hours with Turrie before she went to work, and helping his parents get settled in their new surroundings, JJ felt like he was running on a tread mill and getting nowhere.

If I could just get back to nights, I could see Turrie more and help out my parents during the day, Nolan thought as he eased his patrol car down the main drag, all the while smiling and waving to the throngs of people who crowded the town. But even as he thought about Turrie and his parents JJ knew his real reason for wanting to get back on nights was so he could begin the planning of laying a trap for the Latin Lords. He knew they would be coming for him at some point. *I need to figure out how to force them to come looking for me, so we can end this once and for all.*

JJ was so lost in thought he almost missed the call to return to the station to see the Chief. Catching only a portion of the radio message. He asked the operator to repeat what she just transmitted. Dispatch repeated it and JJ said "Roger," and headed toward the station.

"You wanted to see me Chief?"

"Yes I do JJ. How are you doing?"

"Great, wounds all healed and I am back to full duty." JJ replied.

"Great, because I need to move you over to late nights. Burton's wife has some medical issues and he needs to be on days for a while. I hope it's okay with you. I seem to remember you were always one of those night people who liked working in the dark." The Chief said.

"Well if that's where you need me I am more than happy to help out," JJ said, as he tried to temper a big smile that wanted to creep its way onto his face.

After he had cleared the Chief's office JJ let out a loud, yes! as he fist bumped the air.

22

"It's about time!" Sergeant Keel said out loud as he looked at the forensic report that just arrived back from the state lab. The report confirmed that all the bullets submitted came from the same gun. The ones that killed Officer Castillo, the Delgado girl, and wounded Eddy and the punk gang banger outside of Taft were all fired from the same 9MM hand gun.

Furthermore, they matched the 9MM that was recovered from the canal where the Latin Lords relieved the farm worker of his old station wagon.

Now the task would try to trace the pistol back to the shooter. This task would fall upon the shoulders of Detectives Ernie Mack and Danny Lenz.

Their first order of business would be contacting all the gun stores and pawn shops in a fifty-mile radius of Bakersfield. That would be no small task as there were at least some sixty shops scattered over a large area.

Since all businesses dealing in firearms have to keep permanent records of their transactions, that may lead them to an owner. On the other hand, if the gun came from a private party or was traded between gangs, it could be a dead end. The third option was that the gun was taken in a robbery or theft, but if that was the case, it would have popped up in NCIC, the National Crime Information Center. That was the first one that Mack and Lenz checked which came up negative.

"I don't know about you partner, but I'm going to need breakfast before we start on this journey!"

"I hear you, Mack, let's go over to IHOP and go through the computer printouts over a stack of pancakes."

~ ~ ~

Teddy continued to call Eddy until Eddy finally gave up and answered the phone.

"Jefe, I need to get a new piece. I had to ditch mine in the canal water when we left Taft. I feel naked without it man."

"What do you want me to do about it, you idiot?"

"Eddy, you know I can't buy one. I'm on the 'no buy list'. The cops would be on me like shit man."

"Alright, let me check around and see if I can come up with a piece that isn't traceable."

"Listen Teddy, things are really hot for the 'Lords' right now. You may want to get out of town for awhile till things cool off."

"No way boss, this is my turf and no stupid cop is going to run me off. Besides, I want to off that cop in Ojai if your offer is still good?"

"Oh, it's still good Teddy. I even upped it for what those bastards did to my ride, man."

"Good. Get me another gun, and I'll take him out for you."

"Listen, stay out of sight for a few days and then meet me over behind the old abandoned lumber yard on Friday, and I will have a new piece for you. Tell those two idiot brothers of yours, I don't want to see them around town for a while either, got it?"

"Si´ boss."

~ ~ ~

JJ couldn't wait to get back on the same shift as Turrie's. Life would once again be happy. He had a pretty good idea he was still a target of the 'Lords,' that was just part of being a cop. Besides, all his buddies on the department along with the guys from the S.O. and the CHP where on the lookout for any bangers who would happen to show up in the area. He also was in constant contact with Sergeants' Bentley and Keel over at Bakersfield who were monitoring the Lords as well. He was pretty confident that if there was any movement by the gang, they would standout like a sore thumb.

"Ocean 17, I will be 10-8 from the station." JJ announced over the inter-county communications network.

"10-4, Ocean 17, welcome back to the real world," the dispatcher quipped.

A half dozen or so microphones clicked their approval in the night air acknowledging the smug little comment.

It was exactly eleven thirteen when JJ eased his cruiser out of the parking lot at the P.D. and headed down main street. It was good to be back on nights.

He and Turrie had already planned to have dinner together at the hospital around two, depending on JJ's traffic.

"Ocean 17 copy traffic." The radio came to life.

"Ocean 17 go ahead with traffic."

"Drunks disturbing the peace, parking lot of Ojai park entrance."

"Copy."

"S.O. 2177 I will backup. ETA nine minutes."

"Thank you 2177." The dispatcher acknowledged in return.

JJ was there in three minutes to find a small group of farm workers who had been having a party in the park and got a little loud. JJ pulled up and exited his unit. He approached the small group on foot.

"Okay, time to go home boys, party's over."

"Si´ officer, no problem. We are going now," one of the soberer members of the group said.

"Hey, amigo's pick up your bottles and cans, put them in the trash container right over there," as JJ pointed to a large container.

"Okay officer, we take care of things"

"Gracias, gentlemen."

"Ocean 17 Code 4, you can cancel 2117."

"Affirmative, Ocean 17."

The night air was cool and it was more than comfortable to cruise around town with the window down, besides, you could hear what was going on around you much better. Things were quiet and life was good for Officer JJ Nolan.

23

Thank God there was an all-night Dunkin Donuts in town. It was the only thing open between midnight and six in the morning. JJ pulled his cruiser in and checked off for a quick break.

"Hey, JJ glad to see you back. I have had to put up with that grumpy Thompson while you were gone. He ate me out of house and home and never offered up a dime."

"Glad to be back Sandy. I missed your sweet little smile as well."

"Coffee and a plain cake donut Sandy, I have to meet Turrie for dinner after a while."

"Got it JJ. Glad you are back to normal." she smiled.

JJ wondered what normal really was. If you ask any police officer, the word normal doesn't exist.

He sat with his back to the wall and turned his shoulder mic up a couple clicks. The outside air was cool and dry but inside the hot grease from the fryers made it uncomfortable. Sandy turned on the AC and went back into the kitchen. The next sound was the large window in the front shattering into a million pieces and covering the area with splinting glass. One piece hit the top of

JJ's right ear shaving a thin slice off. Sandy came running out to the front counter, and a second shot rang out hitting her right between the eyes. JJ hit the floor and crawled over to Sandy and touched her neck for a pulse. There wasn't any response. She laid face down with a massive amount of blood pooling around her face.

She was dead before she hit the floor. JJ thought.

He did a fast crawl to get behind the counter for cover and keyed his mike.

"Ocean 17. Shots fired, one dead at Dunkin Donuts! Shooter still active."

His fellow officer in the other beat responded that he was on his way with an E.T.A of three minutes.

JJ could hear three voices from outside approaching the front door of the donut shop.

"Did you get him Teddy?" a person yelled.

"I think so," Teddy shot back.

"Let's check," the third voice said.

Dispatch called out a 1133 to outside agencies. Ojai was quickly getting a reputation as a dangerous place to live after dark. Ojai couldn't afford to lose its laid back reputation that drew in the wealthy and famous personalities.

Officer Nolan eased back into the kitchen and watched the three young Latino men enter the front door. Their faces were covered with bandannas, one was carrying a rifle and the other two had pistols in their hands. They stopped and looked at Sandy's body.

"Where's the cop Teddy?"

"I don't know, maybe he ran out the back door?"

JJ took aim at the one with the rifle and fired, hitting him center mass. He fell onto the glass littered floor and laid motionless. The other two men crouched down by the counter.

"What should we do?"

"I don't need that damn hit money that bad, let's get the fuck out of here," one said.

"What are we going to tell Mom how Teddy was killed?" the other said.

"Freeze assholes or you'll join your brother. Drop your weapons!" JJ said in a loud and commanding voice. Both men complied and quickly let their weapons fall to the floor.

JJ could see the red and blue flashing lights heading his way with the unit's siren blasting away, breaking the night's silence.

JJ kicked their guns away and stood over them until his beat partner helped him cuff them.

"Ocean 17 and 18 to dispatch. Show us as code four. Cancel the1133 and send the M.E. to this location." He put the two men in his cruiser.

The two brothers clammed up and wouldn't talk to the police. They had stolen their Dad's rifle and went against Eddy's orders. The brothers knew they were screwed. Either they were going to prison or Eddy would have them killed.

Chief Olson arrived at the donut shop and took JJ's statement. His beat partner was putting up the crime scene tape and taking photographs of Sandy's body.

The Chief called the owner of the donut shop and notified him that his employee Sandy had been shot and killed. He requested the owner to come to the crime scene and close down his business. Within minutes the owner arrived and emptied the cash register, unplugged the fryers and shut off the lights.

"I'll post a guard until daylight. When you come down in the morning, do not cross the crime scene tape. It's still an active investigation," the Chief said in a firm voice.

It was exactly 3:00 A.M. when JJ arrived at the hospital an hour late. He parked. "Ocean 17, show me out code 7 at the hospital" JJ said and walked into the emergency entrance.

Turrie screamed. "What happened to you?"

"What do you mean?"

"The whole right side of your face and neck is covered in dried blood!"

He looked in a mirror and couldn't believe a nick on the ear could have bled that much.

Turrie washed him up and bandaged his ear.

"When you didn't show up at 2:00 A.M as planned, I was a little worried but I knew you would let me know as soon as you could why you were late."

"I'm really hungry, 'I'll explain everything while we eat, if that's OK?" JJ said.

They walked to the cafeteria hand in hand, as he explained to Turrie what had happened at the donut shop.

Chief Olson drove to the hospital and found JJ and Turrie in the cafeteria.

The Chief joined them at their table.

"JJ, I want you to call your friend Sergeant Bentley at BPD and give him a statement of what went down tonight. He in turn can notify their gang unit. I'll get in touch with detectives Mack and Lenz later this morning and bring them up to date. They can transfer the brothers from our jail to the Ventura County jail. I also need to have a private conversation with you." the Chief said.

"I need to get back to my station and let you two talk business," Turrie replied.

When she was out of ear shot the Chief turned to Nolan. "JJ, I would like to talk with you about your future. No one knows that I plan to retire in the next few months and I want to keep it that way. I did hint about it at one of the department meetings, but no one showed any interest. I would like to see you run for Ojai's next Chief of Police. I will give you my endorsement with pride. I consider you as the best officer on our department. As soon as this current case is resolved with the Latin Lords and the bounty on your head, I want to start grooming you for the leadership of this department."

JJ sat back in his chair with a startled look on his face and unable to speak.

"Think about it son. You have all the qualities that are needed for the job. I've been the Chief now for over twelve years, and if I can do it I know damn well you could handle the job. Mull it over and we'll talk again tomorrow." JJ couldn't wait to tell Turrie but it had to be their secret.

24

Turrie was busy with a patient when JJ walked up to the Nurses' station. The administration clerk was busily entering patient data into the hospital records system. She fought the paper war all night, every night. The nurse looked up at JJ for a moment, noted his bandage and returned to her work.

JJ saw Turrie walk out of a darkened patient room, "Turrie, I think I need to go home, change my bloody uniform, and get back to the office to start my reports."

Turrie scanned the man in the blue uniform standing before her, "JJ do you really need to go to the department right now? You look a little ragged. Why don't you get some rest."

"Turrie, you know the drill. What you do in real life doesn't matter if the paperwork is less than perfect. I need to do this before I forget anything." He leaned into the nurse, gave her a quick kiss, and walked out of the hospital.

JJ eased into his patrol car, sat motionlessly for a few seconds, and thought, *This is not the end. Only a momentary pause until the next time they come.*

After cleaning up at home, he decided to go back to the Dunkin Donut Shop. He needed to see the scene again now that the adrenaline had left his body. There was a Ventura County Sheriff Crime Scene vehicle parked outside the restricted area. He could make out two forensic investigators wearing white coveralls and latex gloves while they processed the crime scene for evidence. He knew they would be there for some time.

The male CSI was walking to his van with some brown paper evidence bags when JJ pulled up.

"Hey JJ, if you keep up at this pace, I might need to get an apartment here in Ojai."

The officer stood outside the perimeter walled off by the yellow tape, "You can't afford this place. It's too much like a resort. Besides, we have zoning laws to keep people like you from staying overnight." He said with a smile.

"Damn JJ what in the hell happened here? Two dead, two captured, you wounded and a bunch of blood. Are you running a CSI school out here in Ojai?" the CSI guy said as he placed a bag of evidence into the back of the van.

JJ drove to the station, and went directly to the Chief's office where he found Olson on the phone. The Chief nodded and motioned to him to have a chair.

"How do you feel?"

JJ moved his hand to lightly touch the side of his head, "I guess I feel pretty good considering the circumstances. My ear is a little smaller than before, the pain has subsided, and the doctor tells me to keep the bandage from getting wet. Other than that, everything is normal. Turrie is okay, but I know she is concerned. She is worried because this is the third attempt on my life, and we don't think it's over. I still need to finish some paperwork before I end my shift. What has happened since I went to the hospital?"

"We identified the three attackers. All three are Latin Lords. The dead one is known as Teddy Ortegon. The other two are his brothers Vicente, age 19, and Rodrigo, who just turned 18 a week ago. They have not said a word, but the idiots carried their operator licenses and Social Security cards. We ran the guns on NCIC and came back with a hit on one of the handguns. We requested a firearms record check with ATF to try to get the history of each weapon. The lab will process the weapons and ammunition for prints and DNA. Their vehicle has been impounded, and will be processed for prints, and any other evidence they can find. According to your statement, one of the bangers mentioned a 'bounty' on you."

JJ asked the Chief, "Will VCSO work the shooting investigation?"

Olson quickly responded, "Yes, as with any other officer involved shooting, they will take it over. Besides, this appears to be related to the other two shootings we have, and the County CSI is processing the crime scene. I will suggest a meeting with Bakersfield PD, VCSO and our department to coordinate this mess. We need to get this stopped, especially because of the 'bounty'. The

Latin Lords seem to be at the epicenter of this whole thing."

JJ agreed with the plan, and went to the patrol office to do more paperwork.

Rodrigo and Vicente sat in separate holding cells, and could not talk to each other, since Vicente was in the Adult male section, and Rodrigo was in the Juvenile section. Rodrigo was scared. He tried very hard not to cry, but he did. He had been in jail before, but not for murder and attempted murder of a police officer. He knew the death penalty was in his future. The cops had told him. He never even pulled the trigger. That was all on Teddy. He needed to talk to his brother. He knew Eddy would be pissed. They missed the cop, and got caught. They had failed. They had been offered a phone call, but neither he nor Vicente had anyone they could call. He waited in the dim light of the holding cell and listened to the other prisoners yelling and screaming into the night.

The sun was sneaking over the top of the Sierra Nevada Mountains. Eddy was still asleep. He and his compadres had partied all night, and he needed to get his head right after taking a cocktail of narcotics a few hours earlier. He was sure he heard loud noises coming from the front of the house, but the drugs in his body kept him in a foggy, dream-like state. He shook his head, but the banging continued. It would not stop. He dragged his half naked body from the bed, and stumbled to the door. He checked the video monitor showing camera views of the exterior of the house. You could never be too careful. He saw a teen boy standing at the front door about to start pounding again.

Eddy pulled the door open to see fourteen-year-old Esteban Ortegon, Teddy's youngest brother. As soon as the door opened, the teen started talking very, very fast, "Teddy, Vicente and Rodrigo went to Ojai to kill the cop. I wasn't supposed to know, but I heard them talking so I asked to go. They had our father's rifle and two pistols. My brothers left at one o'clock, and they haven't returned. My parents are worried, and so am I. What should I do?"

Eddy was trying to process the words, but his brain was still impaired. He pulled the kid into the house, shut the door and sat on a chair.

What in the hell was happening? Teddy and his brothers went to Ojai with guns? Oh fuck, what had they done? How much trouble were they bringing down on our heads? He thought.

"Esteban, what are you talking about? What about Teddy and the others?"

The young teen stood before Eddy, trying to think. "Teddy and my other brothers went to Ojai last night to kill that cop and make a thousand dollars. I wanted to go with them, but they told me I was too young."

"I am not too young," he shouted!

The gang leader sat for a moment. "Do nothing unless I tell you. Go home and keep your mouth shut. I will handle this." He looked at the scared kid,

"You have done well. You have told me things I need to know. Now, go home and be quiet. You were never here. Do you understand?"

Young Esteban left for his house. Eddy thought for a minute, then he got a burner phone and dialed a forbidden number. It was only to be used in dire emergencies. On the second ring a female voice said, "Hello."

Eddy, who could not speak Spanish, replied, "I need your help. Things are real bad here."

The female quietly said, "I know they are bad. I have been monitoring your situation. Stay where you are. Very soon you will receive further instructions." The phone went dead.

Eddy was shivering. Maybe he was coming down from the drugs, or maybe he had just realized this was the beginning of the end for him.

25

"This is why I left Bakersfield," the woman said to herself after talking to Eddy. "A bunch of country bumpkins with a want-to-be gangster attitude and a small-town view of the world. Thank God the Lords are only a small part of our operations."

Seconds after the phone call with Eddy ended, a land line on the woman's desk sounded, she answered it after the second ring. "Ojai Valley Inn, housekeeping, this is Carmen, how may I help you?"

After listening to the concerned voice on the other end of the phone Carmen replied. "I will have someone come over and take care of it. I'll also have them bring some extra towels. It is no problem."

Carmen hung up and mumbled to herself, "Stupid rich bastards can't hold their liquor so they puke all over their $600 a day room. I can't wait until our drug business is running smoothly and I can quit this job."

After she sent one of the maids to clean up the room, Carmen's thoughts returned to Eddy and the Latin Lords. *Thank God, they don't know who I am, and they don't have any idea about our business interests, except for their small part in the street level sales. Still, I need to do something to clean up the cluster fuck the Latin Lords have become. And the sooner the better,* she thought.

Not wanting to prolong the problem, Carmen removed a burner phone from her purse and placed a call. It was answered immediately by Marco with a curt one word answer, "Si."

"I need to speak to Victor," Carmen said sounding like time was of the essence.

"One moment please." Marco handed Victor the phone and Victor mouthed the words "Who is it?" Marco in turn silently said, "Your favorite squeeze." Victor smiled. "How are you my dear?" Victor said in his most charming voice.

"We must meet as soon as possible. My children are causing problems and we need to figure out how to handle them," Carmen replied.

"You're their mother can't you do something to get them back in line?"

"It's too late for motherly advice. I'm afraid I need professional help to deal with the problem."

"Okay.., I will try to help. Let's meet tonight at the usual place." The voice said. Then the line went dead.

"Shit, this is going to cost me big time. Can't put the Big Man on the spot without paying some price." Carmen mumbles as she puts the phone back in her purse. Meanwhile, a thousand miles south in Mexico, a short stocky man in cowboy boots and an impeccably tailored gray suit, had just ended his phone call with

Carmen when he turned to the man next to him and said,

"Please call the pilots we need to make a quick trip to California."

The man responds, "Si, it will be done. Anything else?"

"You better bring a couple of men along. It sounds like the beautiful and charming Carmen has some sort of problem she wants our help with. I think one of her distributors has started to get out of line so we may need to deal with that."

"Whatever you say boss. I will have the men and the plane ready to go," Marco said before hesitating just a bit

"Do you think Carmen is up to the task at hand? You and I have been through a lot together Marco and I value your opinion above all others. I know you were not happy when I chose Carmen to run our operations north of Los Angeles, but I think she can do the job. We may just need to help her with a few problems."

"I leave those kinds of decisions to you boss. Just make sure you are thinking with your brain, not the little man between your legs."

"Now Marco, do you really think I would do a thing like that?" I'll admit Carmen and I had a good thing for a while, but it's over and we have both moved on. One of the problems we had when we were together was that she was too smart and too independent for any man to tame. She wouldn't even give up that damn job of hers at the Inn even though I would have paid her ten times what she made to just stay near and available."

"Like I say you are the boss. So if you say she needs help, then let's help her. Besides it would be nice to have another look at those cha's cha's and that ass of hers."

Both men laughed and Marco left the room to make arrangements for the plane and the men. As soon as he was gone the boss's wife walked into the room.

"Marco looked like he was in a hurry. Am I to assume something is up and you will not be here for dinner again Victor?"

"Yes.., sorry dear. I will have to miss dinner tonight. You know I have to work my love and besides I do it for you and the children."

"Save the bullshit for the children, Victor. I'm not a child and I know you like to think you work to provide for us, but we both know you do it because you love being the big Jefe and having people worship at your feet. You also enjoy your jet set lifestyle including your whores, so don't even pretend you feel sorry having to miss dinner."

With that Victor's wife turned and walked out of the room, slamming the door as she left.

"Women," Victor mumbles.

Victor gathered his things and soon he, Marco, and two of their best soldiers were off to the airport for the flight up the coast to Santa Barbara, California Airport. Victor called Carmen on the way to the airport to tell her their expected arrival time. Carmen knew the drive time from Santa Barbara to Ojai would take at least 45 minutes if not a little longer this time of day. She picked up the burner phone and dialed Eddy back.

He answered right after the first ring, as if he had been holding the phone in his hand since the last time he'd spoken to Carmen. "What did you find out?" Eddy managed to get out through trembling lips.

"Your boys screwed up and you won't be seeing them again." Carmen told Eddy."

"What happened?" He asked.

"They tried to kill some cop in a doughnut shop and all they managed to do was kill an innocent person before the cop killed Teddy and arrested his two brothers. Want to tell me what the hell is going on?" Carmen spoke in an angry voice.

"Teddy's dead, and Rodrigo and Vicente are in jail? Blessed Mother, how did it happen?"

"My guess is you sent children to do a man's work," Carmen snapped.

"It's not that way. I didn't send them. We had some trouble a while back with the cop and our people have been looking for him to settle a score. I guess Teddy and his brothers decided to go after him. Believe me this was not something the Latin Lords sanctioned." Eddy said, leaving out the part about the $1000 bounty. *No use inviting more trouble,* he thought.

"It seems your little gang has had a lot of problems of late and I think it is time we both move on," She answered

"What does that mean, move on?" Eddy asked with the feeling the Lords drug business was over.

"Do I have to draw you a picture, or should I say spray paint it on a wall? I am finished with you and your pitiful crew. I will find someone to replace you so don't ever call this number again and don't ever expect to see anymore product from us! Do you understand? I took a chance on you and it didn't work out so hit the road jack-off, and take your wanna be gangsters with you!" With that Carmen banged the phone down and Eddy was left staring at a dead phone.

"Bitch," he mumbled before throwing the phone against the wall breaking it into a dozen pieces.

26

Carmen started to pace the floor just outside her small office at the Inn.

Not good, she thought. *There is only one way to end this debacle, and that means Eduardo, 'Fast Eddy' Gallegos,' has to disappear before he drops a dime. The last thing I need is for the cops to get wind of our operation. Eddy Gallegos is a liability. He is just too risky to keep around.*

As Victor and his small entourage of black collar businessmen stepped off the small private jet at the Santa Barbara airport, his cell phone rang.

"Yes, my sweet."

The voice on the other end was Carmen. "How soon can we meet?" she asked.

"We are just leaving the airport. Marco is going to get us a rental car under his cover name and we will be on our way in your direction. We should be there in about 45 minutes. I will drop the boys off at that little dive down the street from your Inn and then we can meet at the IHOP say, 2:30."

"See you then," she said and hung up the phone.

Carmen turned to Lupe, her second in command of the housekeeping department and informed her. "Lupe, I will be off property for a while. You're in charge while I am gone. If the boss comes looking for me, tell him I went to the dentist, and I'll be out the rest of the day."

Carmen took off her smock, folded it up and put it in a desk drawer and walked down to the employee parking lot heading for her small red Mercedes E-Class Coupe. Her classy car stood out from all the rest of the employees rides, but no one ever questioned why she drove such a fine automobile. There was no doubt it fit her personality. Smooth lines and easy on he eyes. Carmen clearly didn't fit the image of a Housekeeping Manager; however, it was a good cover for her business with the 'Cartel' and Victor.

To keep the General Manager off her back, she learned his weaknesses very early on when he took the General Managers position at the Inn. She was certain that his wife would not be pleased if she knew how he sniffed around all the female employees, not to mention the little romps in the Executive Suite with her.

Carmen was the first to arrive at IHOP. Carmen pulled into the handicap space and hung the handicap sign on her mirror. She had found it in a room at the Inn where she worked and kept the placard, even though it was issued from another state.

Carmen walked to a booth at the rear of the restaurant and waited for Victor to arrive. Within minutes, a black Lincoln SUV pulled in and parked next to the little red Mercedes.

Carmen fidgeted and was pretended to peruse at the menu when Victor arrived at the table. He leaned over and kissed her on the cheek.

"Chica, you are as beautiful as ever. Are you still banging that boss of yours? The lucky bastard."

"Nice to see you too Victor. I've missed your charming ways," she said in a sarcastic tone.

"So Chica, what are we going to do about your little problem in Bakersfield?"

"Well, I have shut that operation down for now. I am having my team from L.A. handle the Bakersfield area until we can regroup. There is only one person left in Bakersfield who knows about us, or should I say me, and that is the President of the Latin Lords, or what's left of them. His name is Eddy Gallegos. He is not happy about my phone call to him yesterday."

"What do you want to do about this Eddy Gallegos? Victor asked Carmen."

"He needs to disappear, Victor. The sooner the better. He's a complete idiot and makes mistake after mistake and he can't seem to control his gang at all."

"I can arrange that for you Chica, but it will cost you my dear."

"Let me guess, Victor. I will need to bring my knee pads, right?" Carmen said starring directly into Victor's eyes.

"I wish you didn't know me so well Carmen. I will meet you back at the Inn at 4:00 this afternoon. You think you could take that 'Executive Suite' out of service for about an hour?" Victor said almost pleading.

Carmen stood and winked at Victor as she slowly sashayed out of the restaurant leaving the server scratching his head as to what was going on.

Victor cleared his throat as the young server was still fixed on the rear end of Carmen's frame as she walked away.

"May I order something to eat now?" Victor asked.

"Oh yes, ah, I'm sorry. Can I take your order sir?"

"Bring me a short stack and some coffee."

The server quickly exited the scene as Victor picked up his cell phone and called Marco. The voice on the other end just responded, "Si?"

"Send one of the boys out to steal a car. I have a mission for the three of you"

"Go on."

"I want your two guys to head over to Bakersfield tonight and find a guy by the name of Edwardo Gallegos. He goes by Eddy. He's the President of the Latin Lords gang in Bakersfield. He may be at their clubhouse or he may be hiding at his home."

"And when we find him?" Marco asked.

"Eddy needs to disappear without a trace. We need it to look like things got too hot for him in Bakersfield and he lit out for parts unknown. I need you to find an old mine shaft or something like that and make it his permanent place of residence, understand?"

"Got it boss."

When your guys are through, have them find their own way back home. Tell them to ditch the car in

Tijuana Mexico. I want you to meet me at the airport in the morning and we will fly back together."

"Okay, it will be as you say," Marco replied in a business manner.

"Marco.., no prints, no evidence, nice and clean, got it?"

"Got it boss."

~ ~ ~

Shortly after dark, a dark green Blazer SUV pulled up in front of the Latin Lords club house. Marco's two men exited their vehicle. They walked to a partly open door and stepped inside. They saw a guy with his head down asleep at his desk. Marco's man pushed on Eddy's arm three times before Eddy started to wake up.

"Hey man, are you Eddy Gallegos?" Eddy lifted his head and starred at the two strangers who had entered his clubhouse.

"Who wants to know? I want to see a badge, I have my rights, you know," he said in a sleepy voice.

"Here's the thing, Mister Gallegos you don't have any fucking rights where we're concerned." The two men grabbed Eddy by his arms and stood him up.

"Hey man, I don't want any trouble, you must be looking for someone else!" Eddy responded in a frantic voice.

Eddy reached behind his back hoping to find his familiar 40 cal. Smith&Wesson in his waist band, but it wasn't there. He had left it on the couch where he had been taking a nap earlier.

"Shit." Eddy said.

No sooner had the word cleared his lips than one of the men stepped behind him and put an arm bar around his neck and twisted it hard to the left. Eddy choked once and then fell limp to the floor, his neck was broken. He was still alive but paralyzed. One of the men stuffed a rag in Eddy's mouth and pinched his nose hard so that he couldn't breathe. The man held Eddy's nose shut until he was dead.

"Look around this dump, We need to make it look like he left town in a hurry."

Ten minutes later, under the cover of darkness, Eddy's body was loaded into the green SUV blazer along with some personal effects and away they slithered from Bakersfield.

The driver followed the 99 freeway south until it joined the 5 freeway and continued south toward the border. Find a place to drop the body where it will never be found, Marco had told them to drop the green SUV somewhere in Tijuana. As soon as that had been completed they were supposed to call Marco and report in.

27

Marco mentioned if they did a good job there would be an extra reward in their pay envelopes.

They made their way up the I-5 freeways long steep stretch of mountains and started down the other side of the Grape Vine. Before they reached the end, the driver found an off ramp called Salt Lick Trail that lead back into the hilly desert wasteland. He followed the dirt road that took them into a very rough and desolate area with no signs of human habitation. There wasn't any vehicles or campers around. The two men followed the winding dusty trail to the end of the road where the highest hill and rock formations were. They parked and let the dust settle. The driver and passenger stepped out of the SUV and listened for anything that would indicate anyone was around. Not hearing anything, they pulled Eddy's limp body out of the rear hatch of the SUV and together they carried him up the rough terrain. It was 3:00 in the afternoon and the sun was beating down on them. Eddy was not a big man but his dead weight was taking its toll on the two men trying to complete their task. They decided to carry him to the top and place large rocks on him until Eddy was completely covered. Their shirts were soaked with sweat and beads of perspiration were running into their eyes. The lead man stepped over a thin flat rock and twisted his ankle making him fall forward pulling Eddy and his partner with him. They all fell into a large, steep, ten foot deep hole. When they hit the bottom they found themselves in a den of hundreds of Diamondback Rattlesnakes. All three men were bitten numerous times. The two men were trying to climb the ten foot high walls screaming and kicking at the snakes. They had no luck as the snakes continued to strike them. It wasn't long before they collapsed and each died a painful agonizing death.

Three hours later a rumble could be heard from a distance away, echoing off the hills and valleys of the wasteland. It grew louder and louder as four Harley Davidson motorcycles approached. They stopped at the side of the dark green SUV that was there with the back hatch open and the keys in the ignition. The bikers shut their bikes down and shouted out for someone but there was no sounds in return. Their colors told who they were and their sleeveless denim jackets spelled out Hells Angels, Bakersfield Chapter.

The big bearded one had the name Moe embroidered on the front of his denim jacket. He seemed to be in charge.

Moe got off his custom, candy apple red and chrome, motorcycle and walked to the back of the SUV. He could see what appeared to be fresh foot prints of two persons walking up the steep hill close by.

"Wade, you and me will trace these tracks and see who they belong too," Moe said waving to Wade for him to follow.

"You two guys wait here," Moe said.

Moe and Wade were almost to the top when they discovered the dead men in the den of snakes.

"Holy Shit," Wade shouted. They ain't going to need that SUV any longer," Moe laughed. "You got that right, but how we going to ride our four bikes and drive that rig out of here at the same time?" Wade asked.

"The Los Angeles chapter should be here soon to do the trade. Let's hide the SUV and come back in the morning with one of our chicks riding double and she can drive it out. They walked back down to where the other two bikers were waiting and told them what they found, and what their plans were. One of the Angels drove the car down the road a short distance and parked it behind a small hill and walked back to where the others were waiting. The car was completely out of sight.

It wasn't long before the Bakersfield Angels could hear more bikes approaching. Four more motorcycles arrived and parked in front of the first group. The second bunch were also Hells Angels but from the Los Angeles Chapter. The meeting had been set up to trade guns for Cocaine. When their business was finished they all rode out together. When they got to the freeway they each went their separate ways.

Early the next morning Moe and his old lady Bonny, rode back to the spot where they left the SUV and picked it up. They were stealing a vehicle that was stolen earlier by Marco's men.

Bonny started the car and followed Moe out to the freeway unaware she was driving a car that was involved with a crime. The owner hadn't returned from his trip yet, so the car was not in the system as stolen. They headed north toward Bakersfield. Near the top of the Grapevine a CHP motor officer turned on his lights and siren and pulled the dark green SUV Blazer over. Moe went on ahead a quarter mile and stopped to see what was happening with his old lady. He watched as the chippie put the hand cuffs on her and made her sit in the dirt away from the freeway. She was squirming and yelling at the officers.

What the shit is going on, she wasn't speeding or he would have stopped me too, Moe thought to himself.

A few minutes later a CHP cruiser showed up and they placed Bonny in the back seat. The two CHP officers were searching the contents of the Blazer for any weapons or drugs. A flat-bed tow truck arrived and loaded the Blazer on board then turned back toward Los Angeles. Moe found a spot on the freeway to made a U-turn and went south toward LA. After he passed the Chippies he doubled back again. The CHP officers were still at the same location continuing their conversation. Moe pulled to a stop next to them.

"Good morning gentleman," Moe said in a pleasant and cheerful manner.

The officers looked at him and nodded in agreement.

"Could you please tell me why you arrested my lady friend in the Green Blazer?"

"Well sir.., there were several issues. First of all she has an outstanding warrant for failure to appear, expired drivers license, and the tags on the vehicle were expired and she couldn't explain why the registration wasn't in her name. Does that help with your inquiry?"

"Where will she be held?" Moe asked.

"Most likely LASO in Santa Clarita. Were you with her?"

"No sir, I was driving by and I saw you patting her down."

"Hold on Moe, the motor officer said noticing the name patch on his jacket. The officer walked around to the back of the Harley Moe was driving and could see the license plate was located in an illegal spot.

The officer told Moe he was going to issue him a fix-it ticket.

"M-17 to dispatch."

"Dispatch to M-17."

"Run a 28 and 29 on CA MC1268"

"Dispatch to M-17, information comes back to a red 1974 Harley Davidson hog. No wants or warrants."

"Thanks, dispatch, M-17 10-8." (clear)

"Your lucky day Moe, you're free to go."

Moe merged into the traffic heading toward Bakersfield. Five minutes later he pulled over at an off ramp and made a call to Spider Wilson, the Hells Angels top man in Bakersfield. Moe explained what had taken place with the Green Blazer and Bonny.

"Did you tell them about the three dead guys in the snake pit?" Spider wanted to know.

"Na, I'm headed back to where they are holding my old lady and see if I can bargain with them for her release. Maybe I can use the information about the dead guys in the snake pit as an exchange for her release and to have them drop all charges against her."

"Good luck with that," Spider said with a sound of doubt in his voice. Spider never was one who was up beat about anything that didn't bring him money or gratification.

28

Marco was unable to get in touch with his compadres. Even after repeated tries their cell phones remained silent.

It was such a simple task he had asked them to do. What in hell could have gone wrong? He decided to call Carmen and see if she had heard from them.

Carmen looked at her phone display and wondered why Marco would be calling her.

She hesitated then answered on the third ring.

"Hello, Marco what is it you need?" she asked abruptly.

"Sorry to bother you Carmen, but my men have not checked in like they were supposed to. I was wondering if you had heard from them."

"Why do you think they would call me? I have nothing to do with them." she said sounding cold and indifferent.

"Just checking," he said and hung up.

Marco was worried. His guys were long overdue in completing their task and them not answering their phones didn't do anything to calm his nerves. *If these guys have fucked up my ass is grass and I'll end up like Eddy Gallegos,* Marco thought.

He knew if the cops had his men they would be in a world of hurt trying to explain why they were in a stolen car, with a dead man in the trunk and to top it off they were in the country illegally. If that's the case, their biggest problem was Eddy being identified and traced back to Bakersfield and the Latin Lords.

Bakersfield, and what was left of the Latin Lord gang thought Eddy had skipped town and would never be seen again. The Latin Lords gang were a thing of the past. Besides that none of the remaining Latin Lords had any idea how Eddy got in touch with the person supplying their drugs.

~ ~ ~

Hope your boss doesn't mind if we barrow the Executive Suite for a while," Victor said with a snide little grin on his face and grabbing his crotch.

"What he doesn't know won't hurt him. Besides, he is home with his wife and kids by now." Carmen replied as her tight red skirt slid off her hips and hit the floor. She reached behind her back and unsnapped her bra, then stepped out of her panties.

"I love doing business with you Carmen. It's always a pleasure..."

"You are my favorite lover Victor," she said as she unbuckled his belt and slid his pants down and dropped to her knees. He wasn't her favorite. The fact was she only did it to secure her job with him.

When Carmen had finished servicing Victor she went into the bathroom to clean herself up. There was a knock on the suite door. A female voice said, "Carmen if you are still in there you must get out right away. The manager is on the property." Carmen hurriedly got herself refreshed and remade the bed. Victor was standing out on the balcony smoking a cigar. A man down below in the parking lot was staring up at him. The man in the parking lot rushed inside and went to the registration desk and asked the clerk to check the computer on who was booked in the Executive Suite. The clerk recognized the manager and quickly followed his order.

"There's no one booked there sir," the clerk responded with a worried look.

"Then why in hell is someone standing on the suite's balcony smoking a cigar?" The manger shouted as he started for the elevator. He stopped, turned and said, Have Carmen meet me at the suite."

Carmen and Victor hurriedly left the suite and headed for Carmen's office using the stairs. She quickly changed into her working attire. The desk phone rang once as she picked it up. A young man's voice said, "Carmen, the manager is on his way to the Executive Suite and requested you meet him there."

"Why are you late getting here Carmen?" the manager asked seeking a plausible answer..

"I was with a potential guest. He wanted to see our executive suite before checking in. He found it lacking and decided to check other properties in he area."

"You know that's a non-smoking room don't you?"

"Yes sir, I told him he would have to step out on the balcony."

"I want to check the room," the manager said as he started down the hallway to the elevators. Carmen followed close behind hoping she had not forgotten anything when she hurriedly cleaned the room just minutes before.

Carmen used her pass card and opened the door. Everything looked in order but there was a faint odor of cigar smoke.

"Have housekeeping come up here and use air fresheners on this room immediately."

The manager turned on his heels and went to his office. Carmen took a deep breath and sighed a sense of relief.

She went to where Victor was left hiding. He was laughing and said, "That was so much fun. It was like we were back in school and the teacher had almost caught us fooling around." Carmen joined him in his laughter.

29

Moe checked with The Los Angeles County Regional Facility for females, where women were being held awaiting their court action. He was referred to the Inmate Services Information Desk. They in turn confirmed that his lady friend, Bonny, was being processed at the Santa Clarita Sheriff Department, Magic Mountain Pkwy, in Santa Clarita, and that he could visit her during normal visiting hours.

Moe asked to be transferred to Homicide detective division. There was a click and a moment later a voice said. "Sergeant Mendez, Homicide, may I help you?"

"Yeah, I hope you can," Moe said in a half begging voice.

"Okay sir, let's start at the beginning. What's your name and why are you calling homicide?"

"My name is Morris Speaker and I have some information I think you would be interested in. It's concerning three dead bodies."

Sergeant Jake Mendez sat up in his chair and signaled to another deputy to record his conversation.

"I'm listening," Sergeant Mendez said.

"I don't go by Morris anymore, people call me Moe now."

"Okay Moe, so let's get to the dead bodies you supposedly know about."

"Before I do that there are some other things I need to talk to you or someone else about."

"Look man, I'm about to pull the plug on this conversation. Either you get to the point or we're done here," Sergeant Mendez said with a quick response thinking this could very well be a bogus call.

"Okay, I'm a Hells Angel from the Bakersfield chapter. My old lady got pulled over yesterday for some tickets and a failure to appear warrant. She is in your custody right now and I would like to get her released and all charges dropped in exchange for the information I have about three dead bodies."

"Give me your contact number. I need to know where the bodies are located to find out who would handle that jurisdiction. You know Moe, a matter like this could be handled a lot better if you would come in and talk to us one on one," Sergeant Mendez said.

"I hope you're not playing games," Moe said and gave Mendez his contact number.

"I'm as serious as a heart attack when there are three dead bodies laying around. You need to come to see me at 23740 Magic Mountain Parkway, second floor first room on the left."

"I'll be there in an hour and my old lady's name is Bonny York. She's in your system."

"Great, I'll pull up her information and go over it before you get here," Sergeant Mendez said. They hung up and Moe headed for the address Mendez had given him. Traffic was heavy, but in California they allow motorcycles to split lanes. Moe was weaving in and out of the different lanes but paying attention to his speed. The last thing he needed at this point was to be detained by a CHP officer and receive another citation. When he arrived at the Sheriff's Building he told the person behind the thick glass in the waiting room he had an appointment with Sergeant Mendez.

"You can take a seat and wait. Deputy Mendez will be with you shortly."

A tall man with a thick mustache came through a metal door at the side entrance of the waiting room.

"Mr. Moe Speaker?" Mendez said noticing Moe was the only one in the waiting room.

"Good guess," Moe answered sarcastically.

"Follow me to my office upstairs where we can talk."

Mendez opened the door and they entered a 10' X 10' cubical. There were two old wooden desks, four straight back wooden chairs, and several metal filing cabinets. There was one rectangular window at the top of the wall that looked out onto the parking lot. The walls were covered with posters and a bulletin board. When they took a seat, Moe told Sergeant Mendez the complete story, except for where the bodies were located.

Sergeant Mendez told Moc he'd checked with his LT about Moe's request.

"So what did he say?" Moe asked as his eyes widened.

"He said in order for us to be able to get to the bodies, we will have to hire professional snake handlers to empty the pit of dangerous snakes. The LT also said you and I should meet him, along with your lady friend, and the snake handlers tomorrow at Gorman, California in the early morning." Moe had a disappointed look on his face.

"What's the problem?" Sergeant Mendez asked.

"I just don't like early mornings." Moe answered. Mendez shrugged if off.

"You can guide us to the location of the bodies," Mendez answered. He didn't mention the fact Moe and Bonny would not be allowed to speak to each other and they would be riding in separate units, or that during the ride they would be questioned as to how they discovered the bodies in the first place.

When Moe left the Sheriff's Building he decided to stay in the area overnight instead of returning to Bakersfield. The next morning Moe was waiting at the Santa Clarita Sheriff's Building bright and early. He appeared to be half asleep. Sergeant Mendez arrived within minutes of Moe.

"Do we have time for breakfast before we meet the others? I need a cup of strong black coffee" Moe said.

"If we leave now we can catch breakfast in Gorman while we wait for the others," Sergeant Mendez answered.

"Will my bike be okay here?" Moe asked.

"Really...what do you think Moe.., we have a problem around our building with auto and motorcycle thefts? Just lock the damn thing up and get in the SUV."

They were driving out of the city, and encountered very light traffic. Mendez took the Gorman off ramp and pulled into the Denny's Restaurant parking lot. They were the first to arrive. Moe stepped out of the SUV and stretched his arms out and yawned then rubbed his eyes.

The waitress took them to a seat in the back, and they ordered their breakfast.

"Moe, take me through the whole story of what you were doing back in the hills in the first place, when you found the bodies."

Moe didn't mention anything about meeting the other four Hells Angels from the Los Angeles Chapter. He told Mendez that he and three other Angels were scouting a place to have a big party where they could cut lose and not bother anyone. The rest of his story would be as it really happened.

Mendez's LT had Bonny released into his custody.

"Lincoln-50 to dispatch."

"Go ahead Lincoln-50"

"Lincoln-50, 10-7 with female inmate Bonny York in route to Gorman, CA 0830 hours-28,935 mileage."

"10-4 Lincoln-50"

At first the ride was quiet, until the LT started to interview Ms. York.

She began by telling the LT that Moe came back from a ride with three other Angels and told everyone about finding the three dead bodies and a dark green Blazer. He decided to go back the next morning and take her along to drive the car back to Bakersfield.

"What were they going to do with the Blazer?"

"I don't know, they don't discuss those things with the old ladies," she snapped.

"Did you see the dead bodies in the pit?"

"No, I just took Moe's word for it." She looked out the passengers window the rest of the trip. The LT pulled off at Gorman and parked in Denny's parking lot. By this time the four snake wranglers had arrived.

Sergeant Mendez and Moe had finished their breakfast and were sitting in their SUV. The LT called in and reported his miles and time of arrival. He and the Sergeant had left their vehicles to get together for a quick conversation. They wanted to confirm Moe and Bonny's stories. They decided the stories were close enough together that Moe and his old lady were telling the truth. At that point the LT called the coroner's office and asked to have a vehicle and trailer sent to their location immediately. Thirty minutes later two men arrived and introduced themselves as from the Los Angeles Coroner's office. The team was complete.

"We're going to form a caravan and cross over the freeway and drive south to an exit called Salt Lick Trail. We will follow that road to where it ends. I'm sure it will be a bumpy and dusty ride. I've been told it is extremely narrow in spots, so stay far enough back from the vehicle in front of you to maintain a visual of the road."

Mendez and his passenger, Moe, took the lead getting back on the freeway heading south and left the paved freeway to the dirt road named Salt Lick Trail.

"It's about five miles back to where the bodies are," Moe said. Mendez was glad he had the lead unit because of the dust his vehicle was kicking up behind him.

They took it very slow, the five miles seemed more like twenty miles. When they all had reached the end of the road, their vehicles were so dirty they could barely see out the windshields. As the dust cleared you could make out the landscape of an open pasture with scattered trees and hilly outcrops. There was a dry river bed a hundred yards ahead of them but there wasn't any more road. They all exited their various vehicles and joined together as a group.

A snake wrangler spoke up.

"We work in the desert almost every day and have learned to bring a large supply of water. You can help yourselves it's in the back of our truck."

"Okay Moe, where are the bodies located?" The LT asked.

"Wait a minute do we have a deal LT?"

"Yeah, Moe we have a deal," the LT answered.

"Right over there," Moe pointed to a tall rocky hill.

The sun was bearing down and their throats were parched.

30

"**G**entleman, you do realize that those bodies have been there for about four days and I'm sure they are very ripe. It's time we broke out the cigars and Vaseline to prepare for an extremely foul odor," The LT said

The cigars or Vaseline are commonly used by homicide detectives when dealing with decaying human bodies.

Moe lead the way as the group made their way slowly up the rocky hill until Moe stopped and pointed down into the snake pit.

The three dead men were very bloated and sun burned but there were only a few snakes visible.

"They're probably deep in their dens because of the corpses, and the hot sun."

"What do we do next?" Mendez asked.

One of the snake wranglers said. "I'll lower one of our guys by rope to the bottom and then another guy will join him. They will get the snakes to seek refuge in the den holes and bury themselves deep inside. After its safe, the two men from the coroner's office will be lowered down to the bottom of the pit with their body bags. Once the bodies are encased, we rope them and pull them out and do the same for our guys. The rest is up to you fellas," he said with a smile.

The bags didn't do much to prevent the smell of the decomposing corpses. They all pitched in to carry the bodies down the hill to the Coroner's trailer and put the bodies inside. The strong odor still lingered in the air. Everyone took a couple bottles of water and poured it over themselves hoping it would lessen the smell.

The Coroner's men left first and then the snake wranglers were next to leave.

"Okay Moe, you and Bonny can ride back with me and I'll have the paperwork ready for Bonny's release," The LT said. The LT spoke into his phone and explained to a person on the other end about preparing Bonny's release papers.

"I want you to do a follow-up on this case, Sergeant Mendez, and keep me in the loop," the LT said as he and his passengers got into his unit and left.

Sergeant Mendez got in his unit and turned on the air conditioning. He took out a small note pad and started making notes to be used later in his report.

Moe and Bonny left the Sheriff's Building with papers in hand absolving her of all her legal problems with law enforcement. They got on Moe's Harley and immediately returned to Bakersfield.

A message came across Sergeant Mendez desk that the dark green Chevy Blazer that was at the impound lot was listed as a stolen car out of Ojai, California. The owner had reported it missing at the airport parking area when he returned from his trip out of town. Sergeant Mendez had it moved to another secure location and had a forensic team conduct a thorough and detailed inspection on the vehicle. Then he had the sad duty to inform the owner he could not have possession of the car because it was evidence in an ongoing murder investigation.

The coroner called Mendez to let him know what had been established concerning the three dead men taken from the snake pit.

"All three were of Mexican or Latin decent. A wallet in one man's pocket showed his name was Edwardo Gellegos from Bakersfield. The other two men had passports from Mexico.

"But I feel the documents may be bogus," the Coroner commented.

"What makes you think that?" Mendez asked.

"Well there were two over night bags left in the trunk of the car. I had them sent over to my office. They contained men's hygiene products that were made in Guatemala, not Mexico.

Mendez thought it could be a Hells Angels hit on Hispanics for some beef over turf or drugs. *Maybe I'll dig into that later, if need be,* Sergeant Jake Mendez thought. He figured the Bakersfield PD would want to know about Edwardo Gallegos being found dead and if they ever had contact with him.

Bakersfield Sergeant Mike Keel was sitting at his desk when the phone rang.

"Mike Keel here," he said almost sounding disturbed at the call.

"Mike, this is Jake Mendez at LASO. I'm working a multi murder investigation and one of the victims had an ID on him from Bakersfield. I was wondering if you may know him? His name was Edwardo Gallegos."

"Oh ya, he's a bad dude. He was the leader of the Latin Lord's gang here in our area. We thought he was in hot water for some reason and left the area.

Mendez gave Keel the other two men's identification that were found with Gallegos in the snake pit but they didn't ring a bell with Keel.

"We are working with other agencies on the shooting of a police officer in Ojai. Detectives Lenz and Mack from Ventura Sheriff's Office are also evolved in that case. You may want to contact them," Keel said.

"Thanks for the heads-up. I'll give them a call," Mendez replied.

31

The Bakersfield Hells Angels Chapter had been keeping a low profile. Now that they would be handling the drug trade directly from the Mexican Cartel, they didn't want to draw any attention to themselves.

Spider Wilson was sitting on the front porch of their clubhouse when Moe and his lady pulled up.

"My plan worked," Moe shouted with a big grin on his face. Bonny disappeared into the house.

"Tell me in detail how it all went down." Spider said as he waited for Moe to join him on the porch. Several other gang members wanted to hear the story also and gathered around.

Moe embellished the story here and there to make it sound like he was a real tough guy with the sheriff's officers. Spider handed Moe a cigar and said, "Good job my friend."

The other Angels patted Moe on the back and toasted each other with a clink of their beer bottles.

Because the Latin Lords leader and several of its members were dead or in jail, the gang disbanded and was no more, at least for now.

Carmen had already contacted Spider Wilson, the leader of the Bakersfield Hells Angels and made arrangements for them to take over the drug business the Latin Lords handled in the past.

Carmen asked the Angels to expand into other areas in the valley. She suggested as far south as Santa Clarita, west to Ojai, north to Fresno and east to Lancaster. "Those areas have not been worked properly." She said.

Carmen called Spider on his cell phone and told him the first drop would be in Lancaster at a secure location in one week. She went on to say the Angels would need a new family van with current California tags for transporting the drugs. They were to use a clean cut American couple as the driver and passenger. The first drop would cost them $100,000.00 payable on the second drop. Carmen went on to tell Spider they should double their cost so by the third drop they would be in the black.

"You'll have to set up a few guys in the more populated cities to handle the business and resupply them as needed."

"We know how to set up a network. Don't worry, this is not our first rodeo," Spider said rather sharply.

"Okay, Spider. I will see you in Lancaster one week from now." Then Carmen called Victor and brought him up to date.

Spider called a meeting of all the Bakersfield Chapter Members and assigned two guys to each of the larger cities within the Angels new area. He gave Moe, and another guy, with the nickname of 'Preacher' the control of the Ojai area.

~ ~ ~

Both JJ and his parents were now residents of Ojai and he was back working the night shift. He and Turrie set their wedding date for October 1st. They decided that Hawaii would be where they would spend their seven day Honeymoon.

In the meantime Chief Olson began preparing JJ for the Chief's job in Ojai. They spent a couple hours in the afternoon each day studying the political side of working with the City Manager and the City Council. The Chief went over each of their strengths and weaknesses along with what their pet projects were. The Chief schooled JJ on how to run the department on a meager budget and other aspects of the appointed position. They managed to find a secure location to meet away from preying eyes and ears, especially from the local reporters.

During a meeting last year the Chief had dropped a hint that he may be retiring soon. The nine officers attending the meeting didn't even look up or ask any questions so the Chief assumed no one was interested in that position. However he hadn't said anything to the City Council or the City Manager.

The Chief had acquired over six weeks of vacation and comp time. He decided to use it before retiring. Before he left he would appoint Officer JJ Nolan to become the new Assistant Chief during his absence. To do that he had to have the blessings of the full council for the appointment to be effective. That would give Assistant Chief JJ Nolan nearly two months of running the department on his own.

During that time Chief Olson would give his full support to JJ in his bid to become the next Chief of Police.

"He's young, very competent and his family lives in Ojai. JJ is here to stay." Chief Olson reminded everyone.

The Councilmen liked the idea because it would relieve them from putting the vacant position out to bid, and the rigorous task of the city council to interview several strangers applying for the Chief of Police job in Ojai.

When Chief Olson's term would come to the end, JJ would be appointed as Chief of Police and that was that.

The six weeks passed by quickly and Assistant Chief Nolan had become Chief Nolan.

Ten days later, Ojai Officer Gary Jones had come down with the flu. During the time he was unable to work, Chief Nolan stepped up and covered officer Jones beat on the swing shift. The department was running smooth, he stood by his men and they enjoyed working for him.

32

It was Friday, and the annual celebrity basketball charity game was about to get underway. It was being held at the Ojai High School gymnasium and there was standing room only. All the celebrities were from the sports world and other forms of the entertainment world. Together they would make up the two teams. Other famous guests and dignitary would be sitting in the stands, cheering them on.

Normally JJ would be working Officer Jones beat, but not tonight. He assigned another officer to cover it. He planned on being at the high school gym with Turrie to watch the game.

They sat in the front row center court. The high school had provided cheer leaders for both teams and a band to play at half time. This would be the tenth year the event had taken place. The red team had won 5 times in the past and the blue team had 4 wins. Each team was required to have at least two amateurs on the floor at all times. The pros were made up from various players from the NBA. The two amateur players would be famous celebrities from around the country.

Each team wore either a blue or red jersey. The game was in the second quarter when the 7' 2" center for the red team, Tyrone Jackson collapsed at mid court and wasn't moving. The ref blew his whistle to stop the game. The gym immediately became silent. JJ jumped up and ran out to where Tyrone was laying and quickly determined the big man was not breathing. JJ asked a couple of players to stand Tyrone upright while JJ slipped in behind the big man and put his arms around Tyrone chest. He then cupped his hands together to perform the Heimlich Maneuver. Two fast hard jerks and out came a large wad of chewing gum. Tyrone took a couple of quick breaths and waved his hands, telling the crowd he was okay. The whole gymnasium erupted in applause for Chief Nolan's action. The local press and TV media was on hand to capture the whole event. JJ's stock with the city residents just hit a record high.

The next day the media and Tyrone Jackson showed up at Nolan's office where the big man presented JJ with a plaque and a very large donation of $25,000.00 to the Police Department. The money was donated to help the department in its efforts to obtain and train a special dog, for K9 duty.

The Chief was overwhelmed by the gift to the department. They had been talking about adding a K-9 unit and an officer for several months. The request was made for that type of unit in Chief Olson's last budget but the city council had red lined it as too expensive.

JJ dug into the specifics about what it would take for an officer to qualify as a certified dog handler. His research found that most departments required the handler to have an Associate's Bachelor's Degree in criminal justice. The second requirement was that the handler must go through and pass the training course with the dog.

Chief Nolan felt the world around Ojai was changing, and if you looked at what had taken place in the past year it surely proved his thoughts were correct. He wanted a K-9 unit that specialized in sniffing out narcotics. He also knew that various gangs were trying to gain a foothold in the Ojai area.

JJ decided to put some of the undisclosed information Chief Olson had given him to work.

He made a call to Alex Littleton, the most influential member of the city council, and set up a date to discuss a few matters. They met at Mama Holmes Kitchen at 9:30 AM. It was a quaint little place with home made comfort food and special homemade pie's. They sat in the back. JJ had purposely picked a time between breakfast and lunch, figuring the restaurant would only have a few customers . Both men ordered coffee and a slice of warm apple pie.

The Chief spoke first. "Alex, I need your help. The department needs a special officer for our perspective K-9 unit. I know you are aware that we received a donation of twenty five thousand dollars to purchase and pay for a fully trained K-9 dog. The department would also need a modified SUV unit. It doesn't have to be a brand new vehicle, perhaps a low mileage, two or three year old model. We must be ready to police the growing threat of drugs coming into our area and this would be a positive step in that direction. Can I count on you for that support?"

"I don't believe the city could afford that expense for at least two more years," Alex said taking the last bite of his apple pie followed by a sip of his coffee. He acted only slightly interested in JJ's request.

"I know it's a lot to ask and I would be glad to pitch the idea to the city council. I just need your backing"

Alex was more interested in watching the morning news on the TV set just above where they were sitting. JJ continued with his pitch.

"In turn I will do everything I can in helping you bring in that new golf course to Ojai that you want so badly. I'm also aware you have a vested interest in the project, and further more I would promise you I will keep that information to myself."

Alex sat up in his chair and started to deny JJ's accusation. The Chief held his hand up in an effort to quiet Alex.

"Look Alex, I'm in possession of a couple e-mails between you and the persons owning the stock for the golf course. It looks like you are planning to make a large financial gain if the project goes through. It's not a big deal to me and I really don't give a crap, so calm down. I'm just asking you for your support on my project, okay?"

Alex looked like the boy that got caught with his hand in the cookie jar.

"Okay Chief, you'll have my support, but then you and I are even, right?"

"Right. The department will do its part in raising funds for the K-9 unit also, and by the way there won't be any financial gain on my part for this project." JJ said with a wide smile spreading across his face.

They stood and shook hands. Alex knew he had been bested in the game of tit for tat. They left the restaurant and went their separate ways. JJ was getting in his vehicle when his radio boomed out a call from one of his patrol officers.

"I need backup on a traffic stop at Ocean and Upton Avenues. Two Hells Angels motorcycles. CAMC312, and CAMC 894."

"10-11" Chief Nolan relayed to dispatch.

"I'll handle backup. ETA 2 minutes," he continued.

JJ was there in one minute. He turned on his overheads and parked behind the other patrol car. There were two bikers sitting on the curb waiting for dispatch to clear the wants and warrants request from the officer. JJ walked up to his officer and looked at the two drivers' licenses the officer was holding.

"Both of them have minor infractions with their motorcycles," the officer said.

The Chief stared at one of the licenses and had a quizzical look on his face.

"Which one of you is Morris Speaker?" JJ asked. Moe stood up and walked over to where JJ and his officer were standing.

"That would be me, Captain."

"What does my name badge say, smart ass?" JJ asked.

"Oh.., sorry Chief," Moe said with a wide grin on his face.

"And I see by your jacket you go by Moe. Is that correct?"

"Right.., Chiefy."

The other biker named Preacher was laughing out loud at the conversation between Chief Nolan and Moe.

"Mr. Speaker please indulge me and walk to the back of my SUV and put your hands on the window like a good boy."

Moe followed the Chief's instructions.

"What's the purpose of this bullshit, anyway?"

The Chief was doing a pat down search on Mr. Speaker and replied.

"I wanted to ask you a few questions without your friend Preacher being able to hear us." Moe shrugged his shoulder.

Preacher could see what was going on between the Chief and Moe, but couldn't hear any of the conversation.

"So what is it you need to ask me?" Moe wanted to know.

"Did you ever attend Lincoln Junior High School?" JJ wanted to know.

"Yeah, how did you figure that out?" Moe asked showing his bewilderment.

"You don't recognize me do you fat boy?"

"No, was I supposed to?" Moe said harshly.

"I knew you back then. My name is Jimmy John Nolan, and you used to help me with my homework in the seventh grade. We would study at the park in Bakersfield near our homes."

"Yeah, now I remember you. You were a skinny little shit back then. I think I remember I saved your ass from the school bully that was picking on you. We should get together and catch up on old times," Moe said in a more respectful manner.

"I'd like that Moe. Let me give you a burner phone and I'll call you. If you are in a spot where you can't talk just say, "You got the wrong number dick head." I'll understand. If anybody wants to know who was calling you, tell them it was a robo call trying to sell you something."

"Got it, Chief. I'll be looking forward to hearing from you," Moe replied.

JJ marched Moe back to where Preacher was still sitting on the curb.

"Anything you want to add to this fix-it citation?" the officer asked the Chief.

"Yeah, I'd like to issue Moe a citation for being a wise ass, but I'm sure the judge would throw it out."

"And Moe, if you are living in Ojai now, you need to visit DMV and have your license brought up to date. It's due to expire in one week. I don't want to see you driving around our fair city with an expired license. If I do, we'll impound your bike. Now Mr. Preacher, I want to thank for having your motorcycle in order, but if you plan on living in our city, you need to have your address changed from Bakersfield to Ojai.

"Gentlemen you can be on your way," Chief Nolan said in a firm voice.

The two bikers mounted their metal steads and slowly rode away. JJ headed for his office to prepare for the up coming K-9 presentation before the city council.

33

Just to be safe JJ contacted each of the other city councilmen individually and requested their support also. Thank God Chief Olson had confided in him about their little secrets, and the Chief used them quite persuasively.

The request was entered as a line item on the next city council meeting and it passed with ease. The only abstention was from the city manager but the council overrode his vote and the item became part of the budget along with an extension to the library, a new city swimming pool, another fire truck and a traffic light instead of a four way stop sign. These were the things the other councilmen wanted in their districts. Everyone seemed happy. Except maybe the tax payers when they found their city taxes would have a small increase for the next ten years.

It had been two weeks since JJ had talked with Moe Speaker and it seemed like now would be a good time to follow up on that personal meeting with him. JJ dialed his burner number and requested Moe meet with him at the county cemetery. During the call Moe never mentioned their code word and accepted the invite. Although he thought the cemetery was a little creepy.

It was sunny and hot at the cemetery. JJ parked under a large shade tree and waited for Moe to show his face. There were a couple of workers preparing a grave site at the other end of the property, otherwise there didn't seem to be anyone else around. A few minutes later JJ could hear the roar of a motorcycle in the distance. Moe spotted JJ's Black SUV and pulled along side.

"Do you wanna get in the car to be out of the sun?" JJ asked.

"Na, I'll be okay right here," Moe answered feeling kind of weird talking to a cop; not only a cop, but the Chief of Police. Just a short time ago he would have had difficulty imagining he would be in a spot like this talking to a cop about ratting out his brother bikers.

For the first fifteen minutes they talked about their childhood and school. Then the conversation changed. Moe admitted he had made a bunch of bad choices after he left school and started running with the wrong crowd. He told JJ he joined the Angels three years ago and had thought about getting out and doing something useful with his life. The challenge was leaving the Angels. It was very dangerous. He had seen what had happened to others who had tried. His departure would have to be swift and he wouldn't be able to confide in anyone about his plans.

"Well Moe, not all is lost. I think I may be able to help you."

"How in hell could you do that?" Moe said looking down at the grass.

"I would need something in return for my help," JJ suggested.

"Yeah, let me guess, you want me to rat on the Angels, right?"

"You guessed it. That's what it comes down to if you really want out. I will be there for you if you want to go through with it. The choice is yours my friend," JJ offered with a very serious tight lip expression.

"Who would help me disappear?" Moe asked.

"It would most likely be the DEA. I'm not sure, but I'll take charge of that. They are extremely good at that game. I would just be a go between for you," JJ answered.

Moe was slow in giving his answer. He stared out at the rows of mixed gravestones with a look of uncertainty.

"Take your time and think it over. In the meantime don't confide in anyone. Live your life as usual. Call me any time you need to. Just make sure no one is around when you do," JJ said. Thinking, *If Moe contacts me I'll know he's my new CI (Confidential Informant)*.

With that, Moe threw his big leg over his bike, pushed the starter button, with a roar the unforgettable Harley Davidson sound came to life. He cranked on the gas a couple of times and rode off without saying a word.

JJ knew he had planted a seed, now all he had to do was water it now and then and it would grow.

~ ~ ~

Chief Nolan contacted the Los Angeles Chief of Police and inquired if they were going to retire any of their used K-9 units. He felt there would be a better chance of finding one in a larger department than in a smaller one. The LA Chief informed JJ he would look into the matter and give him an answer within 48 hours. Less than 24 hours had passed when Chief Nolan received a call back informing him that they had two such vehicles they were going to recirculate. JJ asked if he could send the departments mechanic to their location to check out the units. It was agreed upon, and the Ojai mechanic left the next morning by plane and landed at LAX where two Los Angeles reserve officers met him. They soon were heading for the rampart division.

The mechanics from the LA motor pool brought both of the vehicles to one location for the inspection. LA made sure all of the safety equipment was in good operating condition before allowing the Ojai mechanic to begin his inspection.

The only difference between the two units was mileage. One had 60,000 miles on it and the other one had 85,000 miles. The unit that the Ojai mechanic chose was stripped of its communication equipment, and made ready for sale. The Ojai city manager was contacted in order to have the funds wired to LAPD. When the purchase was complete the mechanic drove the vehicle to Ojai the next day. The unit was minus the LA emblems on the side and on the rooftop. JJ made arrangements for new communications equipment to be installed and the unit to be repainted with Ojai markings, noting it as a K9 unit.

Chief Nolan sent the LA Chief a note of appreciation for his help.

"Now, I have to find the right man to become our new dog handler. JJ went to communications and requested a message sent out on a podcast for the type of qualified officer Ojai needed. He wanted it to circulate over the entire west coast. Within one week there were three qualified responses.

Chief Nolan contacted each of them and conducted an in depth interview. One declined because the pay offered wasn't to his liking. The other two were invited to come to Ojai for a weekend and stay at the Bradford House Spa and Health Club with all expenses paid. JJ made an agreement with the owners of the Bradford House. He would not bother their place concerning the female escorts that occasionally worked there.

Both of the men accepted JJ's invitation immediately. His dream was coming true. He would have his K-9 unit within three months.

What a great step up that would be for our community, He thought.

34

Chief Nolan asked the manager of The Bradford House to notify him when the two candidates arrived Friday afternoon. The Chief had scheduled dinner with both men at 7:30 PM. He planned to speak with them separately after dinner. Saturday was reserved for a tour of the station and how the new position would work into the current schedule. Later in the afternoon JJ would show them around the city of Ojai. In his prior conversation with the two officers JJ told them what the pay scale amounted to. Sunday was left open for any lingering questions they may have. Early Sunday morning he met with them again and thanked both men for their interest in the position. JJ said he would let them know what his decision was within the next few days. After that they were free to leave for their separate homes, and departments. Both men were single with no children and the move to Ojai wouldn't be that difficult for either.

JJ had made notes concerning the two officers while they were in Ojai. The fact that they each had the educational requirements and both had been dog handlers in the past made the choice very difficult between them. The fact one of the men had three beefs registered against him during his five years of service for being too aggressive, gave JJ some concern. The other officer was from a larger department. He had been a cop for eight years, three of those were with a K-9 unit. The officer was 29 years old and seemed to be a perfect fit for the Ojai department. Chief Nolan notified Dennis Fitzpatrick that he was selected for the dog handler position. He was to report to OPD to meet his new partner, a German Shepard by the name of Wolf. Their new training class would start on the following week. When Dennis was introduced to the rest of the officers he quickly picked up the nick name of 'Fitz'.

~ ~ ~

Moe answered his phone. It was Spider calling to inform him of a small amount of drugs that would be arriving at his location the next day.

"My driver will be a clean cut white guy about 50 years old."

"You guys sell the drugs and send back the money with the next shipment. You understand right?" Spider waited for Moe's response of, "yes," then he hung up.

Oh.., crap, I'm in the drug business whether I like it or not.

I need to get in touch with JJ and let him know what the hell is happening in his city, Moe thought while trilling his key chain around his first finger.

Moe waited until Preacher left to have his motorcycle worked on. "When will you be back?" Moe asked Preacher.

"The guy told me it would take at least an hour," Preacher answered.

"You want me to go with you?" Moe asked.

"Na, I'll be back shortly," Preacher said and rode away. When he was out of sight, Moe dialed Chief Nolan on the burner phone.

The strange new ring startled the Chief, then he remembered it was the phone he gave to Moe.

"Hello, this is Jimmy John," The Chief said

"Hey, Chief, it's Moe. I guess I want out bad enough cause I'm calling you."

"What do you have for me Moe?"

"The leader of the Hells Angels Bakersfield Chapter is sending Preacher and I our first shipment of drugs to sell here in Ojai. What do you want me to do?" Moe asked.

"When will they be here?"

"Tomorrow I suppose."

"How will they arrive?"

"A white van is all they told me. What ya think I outta do?" Moe asked sounding a bit anxious.

"Just be cool my friend. I need to call an old friend with the DEA to get things set up right after we finish our conversation. I'll let them know the latest developments. You just sit tight and act normal, I'll contact you soon," the Chief said and hung up.

JJ immediately called Sergeant Paul Triplet with the DEA.

"Hello, may I speak to Sergeant Triplet please."

"A pleasant voice asked. "Who is calling?"

"This is Chief Of Police JJ Nolan from Ojai."

He waited while soft music played in the background.

"Hello JJ, it's nice hearing from you again so soon. What can I help you with Chief?"

"I heard from my CI a few minutes ago about a small shipment of drugs headed to Ojai. It will arrive tomorrow in a white van. I figured you should know, in case you wanted to act on it." JJ said.

"This operation is just getting started. It's too small to do anything now. We need to wait until your guy can lead us to the people the Hells Angels and others are buying from. Our hope is we can flip them to get directly to their suppliers outside the country. Then it's a matter of proving them guilty in a court of law. No doubt Moe will have to testify against them. After that we'll have to get a U.S Federal Attorney involved and have Moe sign a sworn statement that he is a member of the Bakersfield Hells Angels Chapter, and is working for the government as a C.I. in this case. Then the matter of changing Mr. Morris Speaker identification could take place. Moe or whatever his new name would turn out to be would have all new documents such as official birth certificate, social security card, driver license, credit cards and other necessary information to start a new life as a different person and enter the Federal Witness

Protection Program then disappear into the parts unknown," Sergeant Triplet said.

I sure hope it works out that way, Chief Nolan thought.

"I understand. I'll let Moe know he can continue doing his job with the Hells Angels without the fear of dealing drugs would be held against him. His testimony will absolve him from those type of charges."

"That's right Chief, but for God sake make sure he understands that his immunity does not absolve him from all crimes while working as a C.I." Triplet answered.

"Thanks for your help. I'm sure you'll be able to count on Moe to hold up his part of the bargain." Chief Nolan said.

"We'll be adding more agents to the case as it develops," Triplet answered.

"It's a must that we keep each other in the loop at all times," The Chief commented.

"Absolutely," Sergeant Triplet answered. They hung up.

Chief Nolan leaned back in his chair and studied the movement of the overhead ceiling fan, then off into space. He wondered where this turn of events would take him.

Preacher arrived home and backed his ride into the garage then closed the doors.

"Did you get things taken care of with the judge okay?" Moe asked.

"Yeah, it was those fix-it tickets that the cop sited me for. I'm good to go now," Preacher commented, as he spit the juice from a wad of chewing tobacco from his mouth.

"I still have to get mine fixed yet, but it's just bringing my address up to date," Moe answered. He popped a can of cold beer open and downed it in three gulps.

35

Carmen's cell phone buzzed. The display showed it was from Spider Wilson. She was in a meeting of the hotel staff and couldn't pick up. Spider left a message for her to call him back. After the meeting was over she started to leave the room when the hotel manager called her back. When she reentered, he closed the door behind her and locked it. Carmen knew what he wanted and smiled a sexy little smile at him. There wasn't any conversation between them as they stared into each others eyes. She did her best to hide her disdain for him. He dropped his pants and she reluctantly dropped to her knees. When she finished he put himself back together and thanked her. She stood up and faced him, looking very serious.

"If you are going to continue wanting to do this, or any other type of fooling around, I want a raise," she said sternly. Her statement caught him off guard.

"Well.., how much of an increase do you expect?" he responded.

Without hesitation she said, "Five hundred dollars a month!"

"I can't justify that much to the hotel owners," he countered.

"Okay, then don't bother me again. Oh.., and I promise I won't mention it to your wife also."

The manager was speechless.

She was tired of his bullshit. He treated her like a whore. She was making a bundle of cash in the drug business and didn't need his measly raise of $500.00 a month.

The manager walked around his desk and sat down. He was fiddling with some papers when Carmen spoke again.

"There are a couple of other things I want from you. First, quit messing around with my female staff and secondly, if I decide I need to take off work for a while, I don't have to come begging to you in order to do it."

His face became flush and his lower lip stuck out like he was about to cry.

"You make it sound like you're the manager here," he answered in a defiant voice.

"I don't have the official title, but I've got enough shit on you that you better not make any waves," she shot back.

"You wouldn't dare," he shouted.

"Go ahead and try me, asshole," I'm not afraid of your punk ass," Carmen said with eyes narrowed and flashing darts of anger at him. She stood her ground with her fists clinched, and ready for battle.

The manager stepped back and didn't answer her. He knew she was extremely mad and it would be best to leave her alone. Carmen turned her back to him and walked out of his office smiling a smile of confidence and victory!

Carmen returned Spiders call.

"Hey, Spider I was in a meeting and was unable to take your call. What do you need?"

"I wanted you to know we have our network completely setup and will need another drop twice the size of the first one," he said with pride.

"Great, I'll let you know when it is ready for pick up," she responded. They hung up.

36

Chief Nolan was anxious to see how the K-9 training was coming along. He decided to schedule a one day trip to Moor-Park, California for Turrie and himself. He wanted to view the K-9 training center there. It was a mere 56 miles one way. He figured they could leave early in the morning, watch the training, have lunch and drive home by 2:30 PM the same day. Turrie had arranged for the day off from work the day before so she would be rested for the trip.

They left at 7:00 AM and stopped a little later for breakfast at a small diner along the way. The weather was perfect, not a cloud in the sky and light traffic. JJ used his GPS to guide them directly to the entrance of the training center. There were bleachers in back of the chain link fence that viewed the training field.. They could see the entire field from their location. JJ had worn civilian clothes along with a ball cap and sun glasses. He didn't want his new officer, Dennis Fitzpatrick, to recognize him for fear of making him nervous during his turn with Wolf.

The instructor brought all of the handlers and their dogs close to where JJ and Turrie were sitting, and had the teams go through the different commands. Fitz and Wolf worked well together. Turrie broke out an umbrella to shade them from the bright sun overhead. After the training exercise was over JJ yelled across the field to Fitz and motioned him over to the fence. Fitz brought Wolf through the gate and over to where the Chief and Turrie were standing.

"Hey Chief, what's up?" Fitz said.

"Let me introduce you to my soon to be bride, Turrie." Fitz reached out his hand and said, "Nice to meet you ma'am."

Turrie hesitated and asked if the dog would mind if she touched Fitz hand.

"He'll be fine. In fact you can pet him if you want to." Turrie knelt down and petted Wolf.

"How's the training going?" the Chief asked. "Very well, sir. He's a wonderful dog and we get along extremely well together."

"That's great news. The department can't wait until you both are part of our team."

"I'm looking forward to that too. I have to get back to business now. See you later Chief, and nice to have met you Turrie."

Fitz and Wolf ran back to the training field.

"It's 11:00 o'clock. Are you ready for lunch yet sweetie?" JJ asked.

"Let's start back toward home and we can catch something along the way," Turrie suggested. Their day was relaxed and laid back. It seemed like a world away from their normal daily stress. They both agreed that it was something special to watch the dog handlers put their partners through the various commands.

"It's nice to be able to get away from the hospital, even for a day," Turri said as she adjusted her seat to a reclining position and closed her eyes. Thirty minutes later JJ pulled into a restaurant parking lot and went over a speed bump that woke Turrie from her nap. She sat up and rubbed her eyes.

"Wow, I didn't know I was that tired. Where are we?" Turrie asked as she smiled.

"About half way home," JJ responded.

Turrie looked into the mirror on the back of the visor and fluffed her hair a bit.

"I'm hungry," she said and rubbed her tummy.

It was 2;30 PM when they arrived home. JJ checked in with dispatch hoping that nothing had happened in his absence.

"All's quiet Chief. It's like everyone decided to conduct themselves properly while you were gone," dispatch answered.

"I'll be at home if you need to get in touch," the Chief said.

"You look tired honey, I think we should both take a nap. Remember, I have to go to work at eleven PM. Turrie said.

"Oh.., yeah," he managed to say before she grabbed his belt buckle and pulled him into the bedroom.

"The nap can wait for a few more minutes," she said while peeling off her clothes.

JJ followed her lead, smiling and thinking how lucky he was.

37

Spider got word that a couple of former Latin Lords were making noises about starting up a new gang and challenging the Angels for the Bakersfield drug trade. He called his right hand man and another guy to find those punks and take care of them. Spider didn't want their deaths tied to the Hells Angels in any way. He insisted the Angels keep a low profile.

Spider's right hand guy was named Charley Luna, who had picked up the nickname of Nubbs, a few years back in Los Angeles.

The story goes that Charley had the hots for some chick who rode with a rival biker gang. He got caught one night on their turf banging her. The rival gang proceeded to take them to their clubhouse and cut off four of his fingers at the second knuckle on the left hand. It was a message for other bikers to keep their hands off of the gang's women. The lady was punished by passing her around to all the gang members that night. She was raped over and over. Charley said the next day she got her hands a gun and killed herself.

Nubbs and his partner took one of the cars from the club's inventory and drove around the city looking for another car to steal. After they found what they were looking for, they drove both cars to the city's stockyards and left their vehicle there. Using the stolen car they started their search for the two guys who were trying to start up a new Mexican gang.

Spider didn't want any motorcycles involved or any evidence left that would point to the Angels being involved in the hit.

It was 9:30 PM when they located the two guys in a bar on the south edge of town. Nubbs and his partner sat in the stolen car and waited for them. Two hours had passed before the wanna be new gang leaders exited the bar. Nubbs and his partner snuck up behind the two Hispanic men before they got in their car and hit them hard over the heads with sawed off ball bats knocking them unconscious. They quickly placed plastic bags over their heads and tied them tight, then duct-taped their hands behind their backs.

Nubbs brought their vehicle over to where the two guys lay on the ground, opened the trunk and put them inside along with the ball bats. The two Hells Angels got in and left the scene without anyone noticing what had taken place in the parking lot. They drove north for a hundred miles and buried the dead bodies somewhere in the desert. They returned to the city and picked up their car and dumped the stolen one at the stockyards. Nubbs wiped it clean to make sure no fingerprints or evidence was left and just to be sure he set it on fire.

When they got back to the clubhouse Nubbs reported to Spider that all went well and the problem was taken care of. Spider noticed Nubbs was wearing a new watch and asked him about it.

"Oh.., it's just a souvenir, that's all," Nubbs said with an evil smile.

Seventy two hours later the parents of the two dead men reported them missing. The information crossed Sergeant Keel's desk. Both men had a long rap sheet with Bakersfield PD, as part of the old Latin Lords gang. Keel decided to handle this on his own. The missing person's report gave the parent's address.

Sounds like a good place to start, he thought.

Keel stopped at 705 Beacon Street and walked to the door and rang the bell. A little girl answered the door.

"Is your daddy here?" he asked.

"He no come home no more," she said in broken English then she ran to hide behind her grandmother's long, faded blue dress.

An older woman approached and asked Keel if he was the police. Keel nodded his head and showed his badge.

The old lady looked nervous and worried.

"When did you last see your son?" Keel asked.

"Friday night Raul left to pick up his friend Lucas Moreno. Mrs. Moreno called me yesterday. He not come home either," she said through her tears.

"Do you know where they were going?" Keel asked.

"Si, they both 21 and go to bars to drink."

"Do you know what bars they like to go to?"

"I don't know," she said.

"Can you tell me what kind of car your son drives?"

"Si, it's a black Chevy Monte Carlo."

Sergeant Keel thanked the woman and returned to his office to run the information he had on the vehicle and owner to get the plate number. He asked dispatch to have all patrol units check the bar's parking lots on their beats for a Black Chevy Monte Carlo with California plate, number SAD 2817.

An hour later a patrol unit called in with the information that the vehicle was parked and locked at Juan's Bar & Grill. Keel contacted the officer and told him to stay put, he was on his way.

Keel pulled up to where the Monte Carlo and the police unit were parked.

"Did you find anything around the Chevy?" Keel asked.

"No sir, I figured you would want to check out the car first," the patrol officer said.

"You figured right my man," Keel said as he approached the Monte Carlo.

"Got a Slim-Jim in your unit?" Keel asked.

"Ya Sarge I do"

"Bring it here and we'll give it a try."

When the officer returned with the slim Jim Keel inserted the thin metal blade down the outside glass window on the driver's door and gave it a quick jerk upward. The lock released and they had gained entry. The car was fairly clean inside, just a couple of empty beer bottles on the back seat floorboard. No damage to the car body or tires. No signs of a struggle around the car and no blood anywhere.

"Looks like they just walked away and left the car." Keel mumbled under his breath.

"Call dispatch and have someone come on scene and dust for prints," Keel told the patrol officer. He shook his head in the belief he had missed something. Something that kept the two male occupants from returning home.

There was a house attached to the bar and grill with an entrance on the side. Keel walked over and knocked on the door. It took a few minutes but finally an older Hispanic man answered the door.

"Excuse me sir, are you by any chance, Juan, the owner of the bar and grill?"

"Si amigo, I'm Juan. How can I help you?"

"Do you know the owner of that car in your parking lot?"

"No sir.., it has been there for a couple of days. I thought maybe it didn't run anymore and they would come back to get it."

"Did you have any fights or disagreements in the bar over the last few days?"

"No sir, all is quiet. No one misbehaving, everyone happy," Juan stated, smiling.

Keel thanked the man and returned to the Monte Carlo. Not long after that another BPD unit arrived and an officer began dusting for prints. He lifted quite a few and took them back to the station to run them.

The fingerprints that were lifted from the car came back as the vehicle's owner, Raul and his friend Lucas Moreno.

There's something missing with all this, and I'm beginning to smell a rat. Sergeant Keel thought,

He contacted the duty sergeant from the graveyard shift to see if they had any unusual calls the night the young men went missing. The duty sergeant went to his computer for a search.

"Na, it was a fairly quiet night. Not much to report. Just a couple of bar fights, a domestic, a traffic accident and stolen car that was later found totally stripped and burnt to a crisp at the stockyards."

"Thanks for checking Sarge but I think it's a total dead end for me."

Just to make sure, Keel called Raul's mother again and asked if she had heard from him yet.

"No, he no call me anymore," she said with her hand over her heart.

Somewhere out in the middle of the desert two bodies lay buried in shallow graves, not yet giving up their secret hiding place. Sad.

38

Carmen contacted Spider Wilson and asked him if he knew a guy in Bakersfield named Eddy Gallegos who used to be the head man of the Latin Lords gang.

"Yeah, I've heard the name. Why?"

"We got rid of that gang. Eddy and two of my men left town and no one has heard from them since, just wondered if you or any of your guys had ever seen them?"

Spider started laughing. "You gotta be kidding me," Spider said.

"What's so funny?" Carmen asked.

"That must be the guys Moe found in the snake pit," Spider answered still laughing.

"What guys?" Carmen asked.

"They were all dead when he discovered them. You'll have to get the whole story from Moe. He lives in Ojai. Here's his phone number."

Carmen quickly made note of it. She thanked Spider and hung up. She didn't waste any time and placed a call to the number Spider had provided.

Moe's phone buzzed. The display showed an unidentified caller. He just let it ring until the caller disconnected.

"This is a bunch of crap," Carmen said aloud.

She called Spider back and told him to call this Moe guy and tell him to take her call.

"No problem Carmen. Give me a couple of minutes and then try him again,"

She dialed Moe's number for the second time.

"Moe here. Speak," the voice said with a tone of impatience.

"My name is Carmen and I'm a friend of Spider Wilson."

"So, what do you want with me?" Moe said still questioning her reason for calling him.

I understand you found three dead bodies in the desert, right?"

"So. what if I did?"

"If I describe them could you tell me if I'm right?"

"Yeah, go ahead," Moe answered.

"There were three of them, they each were Latinos. Two were wearing black suits. They had black hair and mustaches. The third guy was shorter and was bald with a tattoo on top of his head. How am I doing?" Carmen asked.

"It could be the same guys but they were all blotted and sun burned when I saw them."

"Were they driving a green blazer SUV?" Carmen asked.

"Spot on lady," Moe quipped.

"How did you come to find them and there?"

"My friends and I drove to a remote area in the desert looking for a place to have a large party and found the SUV sitting at the bottom of a hill. There was no one around, so we went looking for the owner. We discovered them dead in a snake pit at the top of a hill."

"Where's the SUV now?" Carmen asked.

"The Sheriff's Department has it," Moe answered.

"Thank you for your help," Carmen said and hung up.

Carmen called Victor and told him who Moe was and repeated his story.

"Tell Marco what happened to his two men. He'll be happy to know his guys didn't screw up and tell the cops anything."

"Thank you for the information," Victor said with a sigh.

Moe sat in his apartment alone and wondered who this woman Carmen was and why Spider had given her his phone number. He also wasn't clear on how she was involved with the dead guys.

JJ was in his office when Moe called him. Moe was almost in a state of panic.

"Do you know any woman named Carmen?" he asked.

"No, should I?" JJ responded.

"I just thought I would check. I just got off the phone with her. She's asking me all these questions about the three dead bodies I discovered and the green

SUV that was there at the scene. She seemed to know each of the dead guys but I don't know how," Moe said.

"Did you get her number by any chance?"

"Na, it didn't come up on my display."

"How did she get your number?" JJ asked.

"She said Spider Wilson gave it to her."

"Maybe you should give Spider a call to verify it. If he said he did, ask him who she is."

"Okay I'll call him right now, I'll let you know what he has to say." They hung up.

Spider answered on the third ring.

"Hey, Moe what do you need?"

"Boss I just got off the phone with that broad Carmen. She was full of questions and she said you gave her my number."

"Yeah, I did."

"Who the fuck is she anyhow?"

"You really don't need to know now do you Moe?"

"Yeah.., you're right boss, but she must really have some juice for you to give out my number."

"Don't worry about it, my friend. She's just someone we do business with," Spider said and hung up.

He repeated, Spiders line. *Someone we do business with. The only people we do business with are other gangs or drug dealers,* Moe thought. As far as he knew.

39

Moe called JJ again and told him Spider said Carmen was a person the Hells Angels did business with.

"Who is your cell phone carrier?"

"Ocean Cellular," Moe answered.

"Okay, I'll see if I can work some magic and find out who called you or where the call originated from," JJ said sounding hopeful but knowing he was on the edge of committing a crime.

JJ made a call to a friend and asked him to find out where the call came from, and if possible, who the caller was.

"Well Chief, it's possible, but not completely legal. It depends on the circumstance. Let me check it out and call you back."

A few minutes later the Chief's friend returned the call.

"I can't give you the name of the person or the number that made the call, but I can tell you it came from The Ojai Valley Inn."

"That's just five blocks from here," The Chief said.

"I hope that helps you with whatever is going on," the friend said and hung up.

JJ walked outside to get a breath of fresh air and pondered the name Carmen. It sounded like a Hispanic name and there were quite a few Hispanics that worked at The Ojai Valley Inn.

I wonder how many are named Carmen. JJ thought. He continued to ponder the question about the Ojai Valley Inn. Moe's call could also have been from a guest staying there or a delivery person that made the call while at the Inn. He wished his friend could have been able to give him more information like the person's last name. It would have made things so much easier.

JJ was aware that one of his officers had a son who worked at the Inn as a waiter. JJ left a message with dispatch that when Hector Morales came on duty he was to contact the Chief.

In the meantime, he contacted DEA Sergeant Paul Triplet and brought him up to date with the woman named Carmen and her call to Moe. JJ told Sergeant Triplet he also found out that the call originated from the Ojai Valley Inn.

"Maybe now we're getting somewhere," Triplet said. "Keep working it without letting her know you are looking at her. I'll run the first name on NCIC to see if anyone in our area turns up."

"Sounds good. I'll catch you later," JJ said before hanging up.

Triplet ran the name both local and NCIC. Nothing showed up, not even a speeding citation.

"We need more information on this individual because what we have gives us squat," Sergeant Triplet said to a fellow officer who was standing next to him. His hope was that Chief Nolan would be able to get a last name or something.

Carmen was sitting in her housekeeping office at the Inn feeling relieved that the mystery of Eddy Gallegos and Marco's men had been solved. They were no longer a threat to exposing Victor's drug cartel business. She was also happy that her name hadn't surfaced in all of this.

Things should settle down now that the Hells Angels have their network set up; or so she thought.

Hector Morales knocked on the open door of the Chief's office. JJ looked up and invited officer Morales in and asked him to take a seat.

Hector had a worried look on his face.

"Am I in trouble Chief?" Hector asked.

"Not at all, I'm working on something and I think your son may be able to help," JJ said with a smile.

"Is he in trouble?"

"No, no one is in trouble. I just want to ask your son, Johnny, a couple of questions about the staff at the Ojai Valley Inn, and I wanted you to know about it ahead of time. That's all."

"Oh.., I'm sure he will help you if he can Chief."

"Is he working today?"

"Yes sir, he is. Do you want me to call him?"

"That won't be necessary, Hector. I'll contact him later. Thanks for stopping by," JJ said while standing to shake officer Morales hand.

Later that afternoon JJ left the office and went home to change out of his uniform and into civilian clothes and switch to his own personal car. He drove out to the Ojai Valley Inn and waited until he saw Johnny Morales walking toward his car. JJ pulled up along side, rolled down his window and asked Johnny to get in his car and follow him. They stopped at the park where JJ had been shot.

"What going on Chief?"

"I need your help, and you must not tell anyone we talked. Do you understand?"

"Sure, what is it you need?" Johnny asked.

"This may seem silly to you, but it is very important to me. Do you know anyone working at the Inn with the first name Carmen?"

"Oh.., is that all?" Johnny said with a wide smile.

"Yeah, there are two of them. One is in charge of housekeeping and the other one is the Inn's bookkeeper. The one in housekeeping flirts with me and she is sexier than hell, but she is old enough to be my mother. She's got a great body for her age and, oh ya, she drives a red Mercedes Sport coupe. The other one stays in her office most of the time. I don't see her that often," Johnny said.

"Thanks Johnny, remember don't let this conversation get back to either one of them or anyone else for that matter."

"Don't worry Chief, I won't say a word."

JJ headed back to his office and picked up his long range camera. He wanted some shots of Carmen and her red Mercedes. At this moment he was totally stumped on how he could get the other Carmen's photograph.

JJ went back to the Inn's parking lot and continued watching the little red Mercedes until six o'clock. He called in her plate number and it came back to a Arnold Smith out of Fullerton, California, but it wasn't listed as stolen. Must be the plate was switched JJ thought.

Several workers appeared coming out the side door of the Inn. He looked through the camera lens and got a close up of a lady in her mid to late fifties that fit Carmen's description. She was heading for the red Mercedes. JJ snapped several shots of the sexy Hispanic lady.

As Carmen drove away, JJ was just far enough behind that she wouldn't suspect she was being tailed. JJ was hoping she would lead him to her home where he could obtain an address.

Tomorrow he would contact his friend Sergeant Triplet at the DEA and send him the photographs of Carmen to see if they would have any luck running them through their facial recognition program.

Carmen pulled into the driveway of a two story apartment building on 409 Spur Street. She reached out and put her electronic card in the metered slot. The gate lifted and she disappeared into the underground garage. JJ was unable to gain entrance fast enough to get her apartment number. He went to the front entrance and looked at the gang mail box on the wall. Some of the boxes had names on them and others didn't. There wasn't any Carmen listed. JJ heard someone coming down the metal stairs. He turned and walked away from the mail boxes and stood where he could still see them. It was Carmen coming to check her mail. JJ spotted the box she opened and he quickly walked away from the building.

I'll wait until the coast is clear then check for the number on the box, He thought.

An hour had gone by before JJ returned. The box he saw her open was number 207. Now he had a complete address to give to the DEA. The only thing missing was a last name.

JJ decided to call Johnny Morales one more time.

"Did the information I gave you work out okay Chief?" Johnny asked.

"Yes, it gave me everything except a last name and that is why I'm calling. Could you do me one more favor?"

"Sure Chief." Johnny responded

"Do the employees use a time card to punch in and out at the Inn?"

"Yes sir we do," Johnny answered.

"Could you check the last name on each of the two Carmen's time cards and let me know what you come up with?"

"Consider it done Chief. I'll call you when I have the information," Johnny said.

40

Moe's cell phone buzzed and he recognized the name on the display as one of the Hells Angeles in Bakersfield.

"Hey Squirrel, what do ya need?"

"Well Moe, seeing you are staying in Ojai now, I was wondering if you would mind if I take up with your old lady?"

Moe thought for a minute and responded. "That's fine with me. I got my eye on a chic over here I would like to get close to anyway," Moe answered.

Moe really didn't have anyone in Ojai but he thought if he was going into the witness program it would be easier moving around if he was by himself.

"Go ahead Squirrel, treat her well. She's a nice woman and a good lay."

"Yeah, I already found that out," Squirrel said with a laugh. They hung up.

Two days had gone by since JJ had heard from Johnny Morales. That worried the Chief. He hoped Johnny hadn't been caught checking the time cards. He decided to wait one more day before contacting him. Late in the afternoon Johnny called the Chief.

"Hey Chief, I got the last names for you. I had to be careful. The time clock is right beside the bookkeepers office and from her desk she can see when people use it."

"Are you sure you're okay and not in any kind of trouble?" JJ asked.

"Ya, I"m fine. Here are the names you've been waiting for. The one that works as a bookkeeper is Zimmerman and the lady in housekeeping is Perez."

"That's great Johnny. I owe you one," JJ said and they hung up.

In the morning Turrie had finished her shift and arrived home. JJ fixed her breakfast. They talked for a few minutes while Turrie finished her coffee.

"Honey, is there any chance you can switch to days,?" JJ asked with a pleading look.

"I've been watching for an opening, and I think there will be one next month. I know I'm first in line for it," she answered with a sleepy expression on her face.

"Go ahead and hit the sack, I'll clean up the kitchen sweetheart." JJ knew working the night shift always seemed odd that when you arrived home it was still dark and the sun was just beginning to make its appearance. The sun broke over the mountains and a new day was at hand.

On his way to work JJ was thinking to himself what a great life he had. He pulled up to his reserved parking spot and entered the station's back door. He walked directly to his office. JJ passed the coffee machine and could tell by the smell it was from yesterday, so he kept on going. There was a stack of papers that greeted him at his desk. That was the only thing he disliked about his job. When he finished with the paperwork he got in touch with Sergeant Triplet and gave him an update of all the new information he had concerning Carmen.

JJ was hoping that now something would show up in her background.

Spider Wilson was busy putting a deal together between the Angels and another gang in Vancouver BC, Canada who was shopping for a large order of white powder heroin. The buy would have to go through Carmen. She would get Victor's approval and make the necessary arrangements. She called Victor and explained the request. He was skeptical on how Spider would be able to pay up front for it. Victor only dealt in black tar heroin which meant he would have to get the white powder heroin through another source.

He asked Carmen to get additional information before he would make a decision.

Carmen contacted Spider again and relayed Victor's concerns without letting Spider know who the big man was or where he was located. Carmen was outside her workplace sitting in her red Mercedes while talking to Spider. She didn't want to take any chance on her conversation being overheard.

"Tell your boss not to worry. We will pay cash for the shipment. We need 3 kilos of high grade, uncut, white heroin as quick as you can arrange it."

When Victor makes the purchase, he will add his profit and then again when Spider buys it he will double his cost making the Vancouver gang's price quite high. But they know the end users will pay any price to get their hands on it.

"Our man will pick up the order at your warehouse in Lancaster. You can let me know when it arrives and the price," Spider said.

"I'll contact the big man and give him your message," Carmen answered.

JJ was very curious about how Carmen Perez was involved with the Hells Angels. He decided to keep tract of her. He already knew she worked 9 to 5 at the Inn, but what she did on the weekends or nights might lead them to another place all together.

Early Saturday morning JJ parked his car across the street and down the block from her apartment building and waited. At noon he left his stakeout to get lunch at the Burger King a block away. He went inside and stood in line to place his order. JJ looked out the window and noticed a red Mercedes pull into the drive thru lane with one person in it.

Shit, that has to be her, he said to himself. He left the line and went back outside, got in his car and waited for her to make it through the drive up. When she pulled onto the street he fell in behind her and eased back a couples of cars.

If she got her lunch to go maybe she's taking it home, but that can't be because we're heading in the wrong direction. He said to himself.

JJ continued to stay on her tail. A short time later she stopped at a city park and walked toward a picnic table where there was an elderly man sitting on the table bench. He looked old and frail and made an attempt to stand when she drew near. Carmen hugged him and kissed him on the cheek. They sat down and she reached into the Burger King bag and set out the items she had purchased. JJ parked a couple hundred feet away and was using his binoculars to watch the couple. A woman and a empty wheelchair were at the table next to them. A handicap van with no markings on it was parked with its cargo door open in the parking space beside her.

JJ wondered what the connection was between Carmen and the old man.

Perhaps it was her father, he thought.

When they finished their lunch, Carmen gestured with her hand and the woman at the next table got up and brought the wheelchair over to where the old man was sitting and helped him into it. Carmen again kissed the man on the cheek and watched the woman put him on the lift and into the van. She waved goodbye to him as the van left the area.

JJ wrote down the van's license plate number as it sped away. The plate came back to Mary Groves who was a licensed caregiver working out of her home in Ojai. JJ went through the files of the businesses requiring city licenses and found that Mary Groves care giving business has been ongoing for the past 18 years without any complaints or law suits against her.

JJ called Boris Milosevic, the city health inspector to ask a favor.

"Mister Milosevic, how long has it been since your last inspection of Mary Groves Care Giving Services?" There was a pause while Boris looked in his files.

"Chief, her business is scheduled for a visit next month, but if you like I could make it sooner," he said.

"Yeah, that would be great if you could arrange it. While you are there for the inspection see if you can find out who it is she's caring for at the present and let me know."

"Always happy to help our fine police department," Boris answered and they clicked off.

Later that afternoon Boris called Chief Nolan.

"Chief the only one under her care right now is an elderly gentleman named Jose Perez."

"Thank you Boris. That is very helpful," JJ said and clicked off.

That must be her father. No need to go any deeper now, maybe I'll be able to use it later on in our investigation of Carmen, JJ thought.

Victor contacted Carmen and told her to go ahead with the deal with the Hells Angels and their cost would be 1.4 million U.S dollars for three kilos. He told her the shipment would be ready in one week. She contacted Spider and passed on Victor's information.

"That's perfect. We'll have the cash by that time," Spider said and hung up.

What Spider didn't tell Carmen was that his gang had an inside man at an armored car company and that they were going to hold up an armored vehicle in three days.

The robbery was going to take place at a Safeway market in the parking lot, in Ojai. All the Hells Angels would be wearing rubber clown masks and long sleeve shirts to cover any tattoo's or other identifying marks. They were to let the guard go inside and collect the Safeway bag. On his exit from the store they would hold him hostage in front of the other man in the front seat of the armored car. They each would have a gun to the guard's head and threaten to kill him if the other guards didn't comply with their demands. Two other gang members would appear and place wheel locks on the front tires of the armored car. They would give the driver 10 seconds to make a decision before they would pull the trigger on the guard being held outside. They knew the guard in the cab of the vehicle would toss his gun out and comply with their demands.

The getaway car was to pull up to the back end of the armored car and load the entire continents of money bags into the gang's vehicle and leave. The gang had been practicing each step of the plan over and over until the five men had their timing down to one and a half minutes from start to finish.

They were to drive to an old empty warehouse on the outskirts of town, pull inside and wipe the car down, change their clothes and load the sacks of cash into one of the two new cars they had stashed in the warehouse, then wait for dark. They planned on splitting up. Four gang members in the car with no cash and the other two guys in the other car with all the cash.

Spider was sure that with the cash he had on hand and the armored car robbery together would cover the 1.4 million that Carmen would be asking for when his guys picked up the special heroin order. He smiled at his cleverness.

41

Chief Nolan's cell phone buzzed. The display showed an unlisted number.

"Hello," JJ said quizzically and waited.

"Hey Chief, it's Paul Triplet of the DEA. Can you find out if Moe still has the call from Carmen in his cell phone?" Sergeant Triplet asked.

"If he does we can pick up her cell number. Once we have that our boys can listen to all of her incoming and outgoing calls," Paul said sounding confident.

"I tried that through another source and I could only get the location the call originated from," JJ answered.

"Sorry to tell you Chief, we have a lot more juice than you. I can get whatever I need because we have a friendly judge who will listen to our side of the story. It has happened before with no problems," Sergeant Triplet said.

"I'll call Moe right away and get back to you," JJ said.

"Thanks buddy.., I'll be waiting to hear from you," Triplet answered and hung up.

Moe's throw away cell phone buzzed, He knew it was Chief Nolan but he was unable to answer it because his partner Preacher was nearby. After the fourth buzz JJ knew there must be a problem and clicked off.

Moe heard the roar of a Harley approaching his place. He walked out on the front porch and waved to the guy on the chopper as he pulled into the driveway and shut the bike down.

"Hey brother, what's happening?" Moe said.

"I got a delivery for you and I need to take back the cash from your sales," the biker said as he joined Moe on the porch.

"Ya want a cold beer?" Moe asked.

"You bet, I didn't make any stops between Bakersfield and here and it was a hot ride."

Moe went back into the house and grabbed a couple more beers from the refrigerator.

"Where's Preacher?" the biker asked.

"Aw, he's on his rounds delivering requests," Moe laughed.

"Business that good huh?"

"We've been busy too. There's something going on. Spider's got some of the members practicing some sort of a hold-up. They do it over and over every day, and Spider uses a stopwatch to time them. It's funny to see them go through their paces with clown masks on, but it's serious because other guys have wheel locks for a trucks front wheels. My guess it involves an armored car," the biker said taking the last swig of his beer and topping it off with a loud belch.

"Where is this hold-up taking place and when?" Moe asked with interest.

"Don't know my friend. Why do you ask?" the biker said.

"It sounds like a gig I'd like to be in on," Moe said quickly trying to hide his interests.

"You mind if I have another beer brother?" the biker asked as he wiped the back of his hand across his lips.

"Hell no, help yourself, they're in the refrigerator." Moe handed the biker an envelope full of cash to give to Spider.

"Does Spider know how much is in the envelope?" the biker asked.

"Yeah, I called him this morning and gave him the amount. What did you bring us this time," Moe asked.

"Weed, pills, coke and heroin," the biker replied. "I gotta get going. The trip always seems longer when you're riding by yourself," the biker said and emptied his beer bottle.

He hopped on his Harley and disappeared down the street on his way back to Bakersfield.

Moe knew he had to get the information the biker had disclosed to Chief Nolan right away. He was in the process of dialing him when Preacher walked in. Moe quickly disconnected and acted like he was ordering a pizza and put his phone away.

"How did things go on your rounds?" Moe asked Preacher.

"Very good. Business is picking up every day," Preacher answered.

"We got a new delivery while you were gone, so we have plenty of crap to sell. I sent the cash we had on hand back with the rider," Moe disclosed.

"Good, Spider will be happy with our progress," Preacher responded.

"Can you watch the house while I go get my fix-it ticket taken care of?" Moe asked with a frown on his face.

"Not a problem."

Moe was hoping the news would be important enough to the DEA that they would check it out right away. He stopped in back of the Ojai hospital and called JJ.

He was excited about what Moe had to say, and in turn JJ called Sergeant Paul Triplet and repeated Moe's story.

"That's what I've been waiting for. We've tapped Carmen's cell phone and found out that a big buy was happening but she was unaware of where Spider was going to get the money to complete the deal, or where it was going down" Triplet said excitedly.

"Chief, I need you and your officers to be part of this bust"

"Just name it and we'll handle it," JJ answered.

"I'll put it all together and find out the where and when, then I'll give you a call."

42

Milo Erickson was the name of the man on the inside of the armored car company who had furnished Spider with the route and the stops they would be making along the way. Milo told Spider that the longest time they spent at any of their stops was four minutes at the Ojai Safeway store. That was because the store manager was always busy with someone or something and it took longer for him to get to his office and open the safe. Then the manager would put the money in the guard's bag. The guard would sign for it and he would be on his way.

The reason Milo cooperated with Spider was his sister was one of the Angels girlfriends. Spider told him if he didn't help them they would kill her and mail him her body parts daily, starting with her head. Spider had also mentioned to Milo if all went well, he would get a nice chunk of change for his part in the robbery.

"If you go to the cops, we'll kill you and everyone in your family," Spider said.

Milo knew they meant it and did as he was told. He was hoping to see a big payday.

Paul Triplet had made contact with his counter part in Vancouver BC and gave him the particulars of the Hells Angels plan. Then asked about the top biker gang in his area.

"That would also be the Hells Angels Chapter in Vancouver," his contact stated.

"We know they have a large and long run planned next week into the U.S. and we have alerted Seattle DEA too."

The DEA in Los Angeles knew the gangs habits and how Spider Wilson thought. Sergeant Triplet was pretty sure the gang from Canada would make their run all the way to Bakersfield where a couple of bikers would split off and steal a van or a U-Haul then put one of their bikes inside and head for Ojai. They had to have a way to transport the heroin on their trip back to Canada. When they rode as a group, the cops stop them too often for the gang to put the heroin in their bike's saddle bags. The Canada gang had done this kind of thing in the past and knew how to get by the custom check point back home. It was relatively easy. They would make a call to other gang members on the Canadian side and have them drive to a remote area along the border and wait for the van then transfer the heroin and ditch the van, then drive their bikes back to the check point and cross the border without any problems.

Sergeant Triplet had fifteen men, counting himself, assigned to the Los Angeles North Gang Unit Task Force. His particular unit watched the Hells Angels activities from Los Angeles to Bakersfield, California.

The DEA had recently planted a deep undercover guy into the Bakersfield chapter. He reported to Sergeant Triplet that Spider had assigned him to be the driver of the get away van. He also passed it along that Spider had a guy on the inside working for the armored car company. There were four employees working on the interior part of the company building other than drivers.

When Sergeant Triplet heard the news about a person working on the inside and feeding information to the bikers, he and two of his men went to the armored car company and told the man in charge to have the four people gather in a room and hand over their cell phones. One by one the DEA agent went through the cell phones until they found the person who had been talking to someone in Bakersfield. After a few minutes of questioning the man, he confessed to the whole plan disclosing where and when. He was crying, thinking of his sister and what may happen to her.

Triplet called Chief Nolan to let him know he had all the information about the upcoming robbery at Ojai's Safeway market. During their conversation Sergeant Triplet told JJ he wanted the Ojai PD to arrest Carmen tomorrow at her apartment and hold her in the Ojai jail. They had already obtained an arrest warrant for her from a judge. He went on to say the DEA would transfer her to the Los Angeles holding facility later. Sergeant Triplet also requested JJ arrest Moe and Preacher as soon as they could after Carmen was in custody.

"What is your reason for waiting until tomorrow to arrest her?" JJ asked.

"Because she needs to be in Lancaster to receive the drug shipment today. Tomorrow a few of my guys will seize the drugs and arrest whoever is at the warehouse. If she stays there overnight my guys will take care of her arrest. I'm pretty sure she will return to Ojai tonight. I would like your men to take her into custody at her apartment."

"You can count on us. We will make the arrest early before she leaves for work. I will assign 6 men to the detail," JJ said.

"From what we know about her, she has never purchased a firearm, but I sure as hell wouldn't take any chances," Triplet responded.

"What time is the robbery going down?" JJ asked.

"The armored car is scheduled to be at the market between 10:20 and 10:25A.M. Would you rather be in on the arrest of Carmen or with us?" Triplet asked.

"To tell you the truth Paul, I'd like to be involved in both. We can take Carmen down at seven A.M, and have her secured by 7:30. Followed by Moe and Preacher at 8:00. That would give me time to join the task force at your staging point."

"Fine with me, but if there is any hitch along the way, you let me know immediately."

"Roger that," JJ answered in an excited voice.

JJ called his men together and went over his plan for Carmen and the other two biker's arrest.

He assigned two men to go with him to the front door of her apartment with a battering ram. Two others would block the only two exits from the parking area.

One of his men would park his unit directly behind Carmen's red Mercedes to prevent her from using her car to get away. The other man would direct traffic away from the apartment building if necessary.

"I want her cuffed and placed in my unit. I'll take custody of her and bring her back to our jail. She lives at 409 E. Spur Street. It's a two story building. We will meet in the Stafford Funeral Home's parking lot, 6:45 A.M. sharp. Any questions?"

Everyone shook their heads The meeting was over.

"Oh.., yeah, everybody wear your vests in the morning. I don't want anyone getting hurt or killed!" JJ shouted.

At 6:45 A.M. the sun had already peaked over the mountain when the group of police officers gathered together in the parking lot.

Everyone was ready to go. Chief Nolan lead the caravan to Carmen's apartment building. They each deployed to their assigned locations. JJ and two of his officers walked up the stairs to the second floor and down the hallway to Carmen's apartment. JJ nodded his head, one of the officers pounded hard on her door and announced; "Police open the door!" They could hear some muffled noises from within but no response to their demands. The officer repeated his order while hitting the door even harder. Still no response.

"Use the ram," JJ ordered.

Each officer used a handle on the side of the ram and plunged it forward crashing into the door. It gave away with the single hit and flew open. The three men entered the apartment with guns drawn. It appeared no one was there until they found her hiding in the closet. She was shaking so badly she was unable to talk. Carmen was cuffed, patted down, and read her rights then lead downstairs to the Chief's SUV and placed in the back seat. JJ called dispatch and gave the time and mileage before leaving for headquarters. He would repeat the process again upon arrival. The rest of the caravan followed through the city streets with overhead lights flashing.

When Carmen was inside the station, officers took her mug shot and fingerprints. She was placed in a cell apart from any other persons being held.

43

It was 8:15 A.M. and JJ rushed to Moe's location and completed the arrest of Moe and Preacher. Moe was looking at Chief Nolan with eyes that begged the question, "We still have a deal don't we?" JJ noticed Moe's discomfort and slightly nodded his head. He left to meet Sergeant Triplet at their staging area. His heart was beating faster than normal, the excitement was getting to him, but oh how he loved his job.

Sergeant Triplet made arrangements for the armored truck to skip the Safeway market and to continue on their normal route. The company let the DEA use another armored truck to fake out the bikers on their robbery attempt. It was at that time Sergeant Triplet would contacted Sergeant Mike Keel in Bakersfield to have him get a warrant for Spider Wilson's arrest and execute a raid on the Hells Angels clubhouse. They needed to find Spider and place him under arrest for his part in the attempted armored truck robbery.

Triplet would have two of his men inside the decoy armored truck cab and one in the back of the vehicle.

It was time for the borrowed truck to enter the Safeway parking lot. It made its way to the front of the store's automatic door entrance. One uniformed guard in the back of the truck exited with an empty money bag and disappeared inside the store to find the manager.

Showing the manager his credentials he said, "Please don't be alarmed, I'm with the DEA. Do you have automatic door locks for the front entrances?"

"Yes we do, it's that switch right over there" the manager answered pointing to a red switch on the wall.

"Please turn the volume up on the intercom and hand it to me," the agent said quietly.

"The agent pressed the bottom on the bottom of the microphone. It made a squawk and the agent said. "Attention Safeway shoppers we have a security situation. Please leave your shopping carts where they are. Shoppers and all store personnel please head to the back of the store quietly and stay there until the situation is cleared!" The agent reached over and flipped the switch to the front door locks. You could hear the bolts slam shut.

Outside the Hells Angels get away van pulled up in back of the armored truck. The four men poured out of the vehicle wearing their clown masks. Two took up their positions at the store's front door to wait for the armed guard to come out with his bag of cash and the other two were busy attaching the wheel locks on the truck's front wheels. Then unexpectedly the undercover biker got out of the van and locked all the doors, took the keys and walked away, disappearing into the rows of shopper's cars. When the guard didn't appear outside the store the gang suddenly realized something had gone wrong.

A megaphone broke the silence.

"Put your guns down and walk to the front of the truck. Lay down on your bellies, with your arms out to your sides with palms up! Do it now!" was the order.

The four bikers huddled together at the side of the truck shielding them from the parking lot where the megaphone voice was coming from. They quickly decided to get into their van and take off. They made a break for the van only to find it locked and the driver was gone. They ran back to the store entrance, it was locked also.

"Shit, we're screwed," Nubbs said.

They returned to the side of the truck and were trying to come up with an escape plan.

"We need to car-jack a vehicle and get the hell out of here," someone said.

The bikers were looking around in a state of confusion and panic.

"There's a guy sitting in his car with ear plugs in his ears playing games on his tablet. He hasn't a clue what's going on. We can take him hostage and the cops won't dare shoot for fear of hitting a civilian."

The officer behind the megaphone repeated his orders. The DEA defense line was only a few cars away from where the bikers were behind the armored truck. The seconds ticked away, then finally Nubbs shouted out, "Don't shoot, we are coming out," and they walked calmly to the front of the truck hiding their guns the best they could. The bikers made a quick dash for the car with the guy playing games on his electronic device. Fortunately his car doors were locked. When the driver saw the men outside his car pointing guns at him he promptly fainted and slumped over the steering wheel causing the horn to sound off long and loud.

Nubbs looked around and saw what they were up against, with a number of men pointing their assault weapons at the four bikers.

"Drop the weapons guys. This is not worth dying over." The bikers did as Nubbs ordered. They each dropped to their knees and laid down on their bellies. The DEA agents quickly cuffed the four men and radioed to Sergeant Triplet the bikers where cuffed, searched, and read their rights. Triplet called his man inside the market and told him everything was all clear and that he could unlock the store's front doors.

"Remember to thank the employees and shoppers for their cooperation," Sergeant Triplet said with a sense of relief in his voice.

The bikers were placed in the DEA units and driven to the Ojai jail. The wheel locks were removed from the trucks front tires and the vehicle was returned to the armored car company with gratitude.

The only one that wasn't caught in the snare was the big man in Mexico, but perhaps Carmen will help us with that Sergeant Triplet thought.

44

The lone light at the police headquarters in the Chief's office was burning brightly. JJ needed to complete his reports that would be presented to the city council later that week. He was very proud of how everything had turned out. He had earned the respect of his men and the city alike, and Ojai was a much safer place to live and enjoy.

After he was finished JJ sat back in his chair, put his feet on the desk and closed his eyes. He let his thoughts wander. The first thing that crossed his mind was Turrie and their upcoming wedding. He knew she and friends at the hospital were putting things in place.

On a evening earlier when they were together, Turrie told him about her family and her past.

Turrie was born in a small town of Chatsberg, Minnesota and had just began school at the age of six. She was an only child.

One evening in late December her folks hired a babysitter so they would be able to attend the Christmas party where her father worked. Later that night on their way home her father was driving faster than he should have and when he applied the brakes the family car slid on the ice and plunged over the embankment and into the four inch thick icy water of Crooked Lake. The weight of the car broke through the ice and disappeared below the surface fifty feet from shore. When her parents didn't come home that night the babysitter called her mother to explain her problem. The mother contacted the police, who in turned started a search for them. Two days had passed before they found where the car had gone off the road and into the lake.

Turrie's grandmother raised her until she graduated from high school. Her 4.0 grade average would open most college doors for her. She wanted to find one who's medical curriculum was the highest. After an exhaustive search her choice was narrowed down to Chamberlain College located in Phoenix Arizona. It would take her four years to receive her Bachelor of science degree in nursing. When completed she was awarded her RN certificate.

While perusing a web site on her computer that was dedicated to finding open positions for RN's she found one located in Ojai California and sent her resume. The hospital contacted her immediately for a phone interview. They hired her on the spot and requested she start as soon as possible.

That took place four years ago and now she was sure it all was for a good reason. She met and fell in love with JJ and they were soon to be married.

45

The trial against the Hells Angels Bakersfield Chapter for drug trafficking and other charges had been completed, and seven members including Spider Wilson were found guilty and sentenced to long prison terms.

Carmen Perez was also found guilty for her part in drug trafficking. She was offered a deal if she turned over information on the Cartel's operation in Mexico. It wasn't until she found out that Victor wasn't going to help her escape to Mexico that she decided to help the DEA. She and her attorney reached an agreement with the United States Federal Government on a deal where she too would be allowed to disappear into the Federal Witness Program for her cooperation in taking down the Mexican Cartel.

It seemed like the dust had no more then settled when it was time for JJ and Turrie's wedding.

On her day off Turrie and a close friend, Jackie Peterson who was going to be her maid of honor drove to Los Angeles to visit a well known wedding dress designer. The shop was easy to find and offered guest parking in the rear. Turrie and her friend walked to the front of the shop and stopped to gaze at the beautiful display of various wedding accessories and jewelry for the bride. The window on the other side of the entrance offered three exquisite wedding gowns with an assortment of gloves and vails. Turrie's heart was beating faster than normal. She brought one hand to her open mouth and pointed to one fabulous dress after another. They quickly walked in and was greeted by a tall thin woman who could easily pass for a fashion model. The viewing room was cool and there was music playing softly in the background.

The woman who was helping them produced several catalogs containing pictures of various designs the company had available. The two women used post a notes to mark different pages in each catalog. When they were through they had a total of eight pages marked. The hostess asked Turrie's her size. "Six," Turrie replied. The hostess wrote down size and the item numbers from the catalog and handed the list to another woman who disappeared into the back reaches of the shop.

"May I provide you ladies with a refreshment? A little champagne perhaps?" she asked with a friendly smile.

The ladies giggled and nodded. It was a celebration after all. The young woman soon reappeared wheeling a wedding gown cart containing the eight selections Turrie had chosen. He stopped the cart in front of a full length mirror near to where they were seated.

The hostess offered Turrie one of the dresses and directed her to the private changing rooms. Turrie's friend accompanied her to lend a hand in trying on the gown.

For the next hour Turrie was busy looking in the large mirror and admiring how wonderful she looked. Each of the dresses had a price tag attached.

Turrie whispered to Jackie that the dresses where beautiful, but it seemed quite expensive to only be worn once.

"Oh.., don't be silly, remember this is your special day and you want those great memories and pictures to look back on," Jackie said,

"Yes, of course, but you're not the one paying for it now are you?" Turrie laughed.

When they had completed their business at the wedding gown shop they stopped to have lunch at a nearby cafe before heading back to Ojai. They each ordered a sandwich from the menu and an ice tea. Before they were served a very tall, black man and a stunning blonde lady sat down at the table next to Turrie and Jackie. Turrie kept staring at the man, until he asked Turrie if he knew her.

"Yes, I believe your name is Tyrone Jackson isn't it?"

"Yes it is, do you follow basketball?" he asked.

"No, not really. But I think you know my soon to be husband, Chief JJ Nolan."

Tyrone jumped up and clapped his large hands together and with a wide grin and said, "That's the man that saved my life in Ojai!" Turrie smiled and nodded her head.

"Please join my friend Sheryl and I for lunch."

"Oh, no that is a very kind offer but we wouldn't want to intrude."

"Oh yes, my dears, and it will be my treat. I insist." The ladies moved their ice teas over to the other table and Tyrone introduced his friend to the ladies and Turrie in turn did the same with Jackie. The conversation was light and cheery. Tyrone and Sheryl ordered and when they were each through with lunch Turrie and Jackie thanked Tyrone for his gracious hospitality and started back to Ojai.

When Turrie arrived home she called JJ and excitedly told him about her trip to the bridal shop and the chance run in with Tyrone Jackson. JJ was about to go into a meeting with the city council when she called. He patiently listened to her story and was happy for her excitement.

The meeting was being called to order as he entered the council chambers. JJ took a seat in the front row of the audience section facing the members of the city's most important men, or at least they thought they were. There were three others in the audience. One was a newspaper reporter who always attended the monthly meeting to give their readers up to date information that had been discussed and considered by the council. The other two, one lady and a man sat in their seats fumbling with papers. No doubt they had a grievance of some sort with the city. JJ would wait until he was called to state his business, then leave. He was requesting a uniform allowance increase and new protective armor for his men to be considered in his upcoming budget.

~ ~ ~

Turrie and JJ had selected St. Ann's Cathodic church for their wedding and had planned on inviting family and a few friends to attend. She had chosen her bridesmaids from work.

The word somehow got out to the public about the wedding and and the town was excited for the couple.

Word travels fast in small communities like Ojai. Retired Chief Olson approached JJ and asked him if he and Turrie would mind if he helped by taking charge of planning the reception?

Olson had a great idea and would need to enlist the help of the high school for the use of their gymnasium for the reception location, and three of the major hotels to cater the food. The cake was offered free of charge by a bakery in the city. Chief Olson had enlisted over twenty volunteers to help with the decorations. He also made arrangements to let the whole city know about the reception and they all were invited. The police photographer was handling the wedding and reception pictures.

The only thing left for JJ to do was to pick the best man. He asked the man that had helped his law enforcement career the most. That was former Chief Olson who gladly accepted.

A week later Turrie returned to the bridal shop for her final fitting. There were a couple last minute adjustments. The wedding was six days away and the shop assured her that her gown would be ready and delivered in four days. JJ had rented a black tux. His five groomsmen would be wearing medium gray suit jackets, white shirts with black ties and black slacks and shoes.

Just to strengthen his position in town, his groomsmen were the four city councilmen and the city manager.

Finally the day arrived. Turrie was a bundle of nerves as she and her bridesmaids were gathered in a small room in the church laughing and giggling like a bunch of school girls.

The organist played the traditional wedding march and all the attendees turned in their seats to watch Turrie slowly glide down the aisle. JJ was already in place at the altar. Both their hearts were beating at an accelerated rate. JJ had a warm smile while admiring Turrie's beauty and the wonderful gown she had chosen. He was having a hard time believing what a lucky man he was to have found his true love and life's companion.

The ceremony went off without a hitch. They stepped out the front door of the church to a large group of friends and family, who had gathered there to toss rice on top of the newly married couple. The chauffeur had opened the back seat door so they could get away from the well wishers. They entered their limousine and were driven to the high school gym. Turrie was laughing and picking rice out of her hair. While JJ still had visions of her walking down the aisle toward him.

At the school gymnasium, bleachers had been tucked away and hidden into the walls to make more room for the many guests, tables and food that soon would crowd the gym. A small local band was playing music in a little area that had been set aside for dancing.

At the entrance of the gym were two long tables for gifts. As the people poured in the gift tables were stacked high with beautifully wrapped gifts for the newlyweds. Four other tables near the band were waiting for the wedding party. The master of ceremonies was former Chief Olson who gave the couple their first toast and told a few funny stories about JJ. Then others followed suit. The Chief had set up a money tree where the men had to pay in order to dance with the bride. Poor Turrie, her feet were stepped on so many times she couldn't remember. She was a good sport and didn't lose her fantastic smile no matter how bad her feet ached.

The refreshments were non alcoholic. After all, who would want to get drunk at the Chief Of Police's reception. A few hours had gone by before the newly weds left for JJ's place. Their plans were to drive to LAX and catch a flight at noon the next day to Hawaii.

46

HAWAII

They were flying first class, and the comfort and attention they received on the flight was wonderful. Turrie struck up a conversation with another lady about her own age who also happened to be a nurse. JJ relaxed and listened to his favorite country music station. They were served lunch made up of pineapple and shrimp on a bed of lettuce. Later they each had a cocktail courtesy of the airlines.

Just before landing, the pilot gave an announcement that the temperature in Honolulu Hawaii was 85 degrees with a three miles an hour breeze. When they deplaned there were beautiful Hawaiian girls draping colorful flowered Lei's around their necks. A shuttle took them into the main airport terminal. Taxis were waiting curbside to drop passengers at their appointed hotels or other locations. There were two other couples that had joined them in the same taxi all of them were there in Honolulu on their honeymoon. The taxi drove to the entrance of the Hawaiian Hilton where they were staying. The driver removed their luggage. JJ paid the driver a hefty tip and the taxi departed with the other two happy couples.

A bellman took their luggage to the registration desk and assisted them with their check-in. He loaded their luggage onto a cart and escorted them to the elevator.

Their room was on the fifteenth floor with the windows facing the ocean and overlooking Waikiki Beach.

Neither JJ or Turrie had been to Hawaii before. They had a whole week to explore the island. Turrie was busy putting away their clothes and setting up the bathroom with her make up and other necessities. JJ got in the shower and a minute hadn't passed before Turrie slid in next to him.

"Hi sweetheart," she purred and began soaping his back. He turned to face her and they kissed a long passionate kiss then another and another. They finished their shower and helped dry each other off. JJ put a towel around his waist and walked to the window and closed the blinds. The room was darkened. Turrie pulled back the bed covers and laid on the clean white sheets. JJ took off the towel and laid down beside her longing for her touch. Their lips found each other and kissed softly. For the next hour their bodies were entangled in various stages of making love. Afterwards they were so relaxed they fell asleep in each others arms.

The bellman knocked lightly on the door. "Who's there?" JJ shouted while shaking Turrie awake.

"I have a gift for you," the bellman said.

"Just a minute," JJ answered.

He wrapped the towel around his waist and went to the door. Turrie had rushed into the bathroom and closed the door. JJ pulled the room door ajar and peeked out. The bellman was holding a large bouquet of beautiful flowers and a chilled bottle of champagne. JJ opened the door and let the bellman in. He placed the gifts on the table in the darkened room and stood there waiting for his tip. JJ found his slacks and retrieved his wallet. He handed the young man a twenty and the bellman left. JJ told Turrie the coast was clear and she could come out of the bathroom.

"Who is it from?" Turrie asked.

"JJ looked at the card tucked in the bouquet and read the note.

"Thank you for letting me help you plan your honeymoon trip. I know you will have a wonderful time. Love to you both. Your travel agent, Pam Lacey.

"Ooh, how sweet of her," Turrie sighed. JJ uncorked the Champagne and filled the two glasses that came with the gift. They toasted their marriage and their love for each other. JJ glanced at the clock, it was 6:45 P.M. "I'm hungry as hell," he said. Turrie agreed, and suggested they go downstairs to have dinner. They walked through the lobby. A host stood at the door of the dining room and lead them to a table. He helped Turrie with her chair and placed the menus on the table. Within a minute a waiter was asking for their drink order. They each choose wine. A few minutes had gone by when JJ caught the waiter's eye and nodded that they were ready to order. Turrie choose Mahi-Mahi and JJ selected a rib-eye steak medium-well.

After they finished their lovely meal they walked outside and crossed the street. The city was still bustling with tourists enjoying the warm tropical evening. The pair reached the edge of Waikiki Beach and paused for a moment when Turrie slipped off her sandals and JJ removed his shoes. They stepped onto the clean white sand and walked to the ocean's edge and felt the wet sand slip between their toes. The moon light was bright enough to let them stroll hand in hand along the beach as other couples around them were doing. "It's so romantic," Turrie whispered. JJ nodded in agreement. JJ said, "It's a different world here. It's where people go to forget their worries and relax." They walked back to their hotel with shoes still in hand.

The next day they were up early and went down to the lobby. There was a rack full of leaflets offering things do to and places to go while in Hawaii. Turrie saw one concerning a Luau. "I want to go to a real Luau!" she said jumping up and down. JJ called the number listed on the sheet and made the arrangement for attending the Hawaii feast. An open bus would pick them up and bring them back when it was over.

They had breakfast at the hotel and walked along the busy street to an open air market that housed a number of various vendors. Turrie wanted to have her nails done and JJ needed to buy a couple of Hawaiian shirts.

After JJ made his purchases he headed to where Turrie was having her nails painted. He stopped in his tracks and stared ahead a couple of booths at the nail tech that was finishing up on Turrie. He was wearing sun glasses and flipped them off for just a second and squinted his eyes to help make things clearer, then put them back on. The booth next to where he was standing was selling large brimmed straw hats. He tried one on and handed the clerk the money. All of a sudden he didn't want to be recognized. Turrie saw him and waved him toward her. He hesitated and she waved again. He waved back and mouthed the word, "I'll be right there," and smiled. Finally Turrie had finished and walked over to where JJ was standing with his back to her.

"What in the heck is going on?" she wanted to know.

He gently took her arm and had her walk even further away from the nail tech's booth.

"Why are you acting so strangely?" Turrie wanted to know.

When they reached the street, JJ stopped and said, "Evidently you didn't recognize that woman that worked on your nails, did you?"

"She said her name was Lucy."

"Well, it's not Lucy, that lady is Carmen Perez, the woman who the DEA placed in the Governments Federal Witness Program. I didn't want her to see me, because it would have spooked her, and if she told that to her handlers they would have to move her again to a new location. There isn't any need to disrupt her current location now that she has settled in. And we shouldn't mention it to anyone that we saw her either."

"How can you be sure it was her?" Turrie asked looking at him quizzically.

She was wearing a disguise with the fake red wig and the phony glasses but with the three earrings on one side and the red and green hummingbird tattoo on her left forearm it was a dead give away. It was her alright and it looked as though she was enjoying life on the island."

"Holy cow, what are we going to do now?" Turrie asked.

"Nothing, we're just going to stay away from that open-air market."

"She did a great job on my nails. Look, she even painted Diamond Head on one nail," Turrie said while lifting her hands to show JJ. He agreed Carmen had done a beautiful job.

What a departure from her old life, JJ thought.

The next afternoon JJ and Turrie waited at curbside in front of their hotel for the Luau bus. Most of the seats were already taken. They traveled to a nearby beach front area that was set up just for the luau festivities. The bus passed through a large gate and the passengers disembarked and were told to followed the guide's instructions. There was about a hundred people attending the feast. Everyone watched the Hawaiian men prepare the huge pig and bury it on the palm leaves and hot rocks. There were long tables set up with red and blue Mi-Ti's in small but deadly three ounce cups. The crowd was told to help themselves.

There were an assortment of games to play and hula dancers to watch. Turrie got her face painted like a native warrior. The red and blue drinks went down easy and before they knew it those harmless little drinks were causing them to slur their words. When the pig was done the host requested everyone take their seats in the row of tables. Beautiful Hawaiian girls served the guests the delicious roasted pig and an assortment of other special Hawaiian dishes.

After several hours the festivities finally came to an end. The drivers loaded everyone on the buses and delivered the tipsy guests back to their hotels.

"Damn that was fun!" Turrie said as they entered the hotel.

"It sure was, and I still have a buzz going." JJ answered noting how pretty his wife looked. They both had mild sunburns. Turrie stopped at the small shop in the lobby to buy a tube of Aloe Cream. When they left the shop Turrie stood facing JJ with no space between them and looked up into his eyes and said. "You know what honey?"

"No, what?" he answered.

"I'm horny," Turrie said with a grin on her face. She grabbed the front of his shirt and pulled him into the elevator and promptly pushed the number 15. "Let's just see what we can do about that sweetheart," he whispered in her ear.

"I don't ever want to go home," she said with a giggle.

The End

About the Author

Former police officer and author R.T. Wiley brings over a decade's experience in law enforcement to his writing. From an urban police department in California to a county sheriff's department in Oregon, Wiley draws on his adventures in the Pacific Northwest.

Now retired, he resides in Chandler, AZ with his wife Marilyn and their dog Hudson.

More books by R. T. Wiley

Snowflake

Seriously Flawed

Martini I

Martini II

Martini III

Made in the USA
Monee, IL
17 March 2020